A Daimon Novella

RENASCENCE
OF THE
FORSAKEN

ELIJAH HER

ISBN: 979-8-9927299-9-3 (paperback)
ISBN: 979-8-9945528-0-3 (ebook)

F90 PRESS

www.f90press.com

*For those who have ever believed love was meant only for others,
not for themselves. This is for you.*

CONTENT NOTES

Renascence of the Forsaken includes explicit sexual content. It also touches on themes some may be sensitive to or find triggering:

Depictions of organized crime and physical violence. Struggles with mental health and loss.

PRONUNCIATION GUIDE

Aither *(EYE-thur)*
Arestis *(uh-RESS-tis)*
Daimon *(DYE-mon)*
Dmitriy *(DMI-tree)*
Erebos *(EH-reh-bos)*
Eryx *(EH-riks)*
Eudaimon *(YOU-dye-mon)*
Jaehyun Seok *(JAE-hyeon SUHK)*
Kakodaimon *(KAK-oh-dye-mon)*
Khaos *(KAY-os)*
Kasius Nikolaou *(KAH-see-us Nee-ko-LA-oh)*
Nikolai *(NEE-koh-lye)*
Philetos *(fee-LEE-tos)*
Silas Vassallo *(SIGH-lus vah-SAHL-loh)*
Theion *(THAY-on)*
Zayd *(ZAY-d)*

CHAPTER ONE

That beautiful smile. It lingered in my mind, a ghost of laughter and light. I saw it—again and again—shaped by annoyance, softened by affection, caught between moments that slipped through my fingers like sand.

"Zayd, promise me..." The words barely made it past my lips, as weak as breath, as weighty as prayer.

"I promise." His voice trembled, his dark blue eyes glossy with something I didn't want to name. His brows knitted, his mouth set in a way that sent something sharp through me—something like anger, like helplessness. I wanted to kiss it away, to cradle his face until his laughter returned. Until I saw that smile again.

And then, for a moment, I did.

That smile. *His* smile.

It was the last thing I saw before the fog stole everything from me. It rolled in thick and merciless, swallowing him whole. I tried to chase him, tried to carve through the mist with desperate hands, but he was gone.

"*Kasius.*"

A voice called to me through the haze, muffled, as though I were submerged underwater.

"Kasius."

This time, a force slammed into my chest, shoving me backward—

—and then nothing. Darkness.

"Kasius! Hey, wake up. It's just a dream." The voice came clearer now, pulling me out of the abyss. I opened my eyes to find a woman looming over me, her wide hazel eyes brimming with curiosity.

Who—?

I bolted upright, only to immediately regret it as my limbs tangled beneath me, sending me tumbling from the bed with an undignified thud.

"Kas, what the hell?" she huffed, peering over the edge of the mattress. Her brows furrowed, her bare chest pressing together as she leaned forward. "Why are you looking at me like that?"

"I—I, uh..." The sound scraped out of me as my eyes darted around the unfamiliar space. A dorm. A woman's dorm, if the evidence plastered across the walls was anything to go by—photographs of this woman with other girls, arms slung around each other, their smiles wide and careless, red cups and glittering bottles raised in toast. A few were tacked crookedly, as if even gravity was drunk with them.

Textbooks sprawled across a desk, their spines bent and weary, pages bristling with sticky notes and fluorescent highlights. A heap of laundry slumped in the corner, lace and denim tangled in an undignified knot. Candles half-burned lined the windowsill, their scents—vanilla, lavender, something cloyingly sweet—fighting for dominance against the sour tang of last night's liquor.

Theions, it *was* a dorm room.

Her sigh was exasperated, long-suffering. "I knew this was a mistake. They told me not to meet up with you again, but here we are." She ran a hand through her tousled blonde hair before snatching up clothes from the floor and throwing them into my lap. "Just go. We're done."

"Okay," I said, because what else was there to say?

I stood, clutching the bundle of fabric against me in a flimsy attempt at modesty. My thoughts reeled.

"That's it? Okay?" she snapped, yanking a shirt over her head. "You were begging for me last night! Or was that just to fuck me again?"

Fucked her? If I had ever stooped so low as to seek a mortal for pleasure in a place like this, I would remember it. My gaze fell to the clothes in my hands—jeans, a t-shirt, a hoodie. Plain, forgettable. As if I would ever drape myself in something so cheap. And yet—

The moment struck like a blade sliding between my ribs. Not images, but memories. Not mine, yet they played behind my eyes as if they belonged to me. Laughter, rich and careless. Liquor burning down my throat, dulling my senses.

Bodies twisting in sheets, hands grasping, mouths seeking, a heat that built and broke into something fleeting, something mediocre.

The weight of it settled in my gut.

Shit.

"Jenni." The name slipped out before I could stop it. Then, just as effortlessly, so did—"Oh... I cheated on you."

Silence.

She stared at me, and for the first time in my long, long existence, I felt something akin to fear.

A mortal scared me. What the fuck.

"I'm going to go," I announced, fumbling to pull on my pants. Before she could unleash whatever fury was brewing in those eyes, I turned and bolted, slamming the door shut behind me.

The hall was alive with movement, students drifting between rooms, laughter and conversation weaving through the air.

What the fuck is going on?

Daimons can't get drunk. But somehow, I must've found a way, because I didn't know where I was, who I was with, or why my head felt like it had been cracked open and stuffed with someone else's memories.

"What's up, Kas?"

A guy—tall, broad-shouldered, with the unmistakable aura of a douchebag—clapped me on the shoulder as he passed.

"Dev," I greeted, my lips automatically curling into a grin as my hand and chin lifted.

Seriously, what the fuck is going on?

My legs moved before my mind could catch up, carrying me down the hall, through the crowd, past faces that flickered with vague familiarity. I smiled at them. I nodded.

I didn't know who the fuck they were, but they all seemed to know me.

"Eryx, stop this!"

The voice hit me like a tidal wave, flooding my mind, filling every corner of me with its familiarity.

Zayd.

A sharp pain lanced through my skull, sudden and searing, like a blade driven between bone. I pressed my fingers to my temples, willing it away, but the sensation clung to me, raw and unrelenting. My other hand found the exit door, bracing against it as I stumbled forward into the crisp, biting air of morning. Autumn leaves cracked and crumbled beneath my shoes, brittle as old parchment. The hoodie clung too warm, too foreign, and I dragged at the zipper, desperate to free myself from it.

I needed to call to Khaos. I needed to leave. My senses burned, every sound too sharp, every scent too thick. The world felt... different.

I stood there, poised on the stone steps of the campus, reaching inward, reaching beyond. Searching for the familiar pull, the abyss that had always answered. But there was nothing. No whisper, no abyss. Just silence.

Had I been forsaken by the Theion?

A hollow ache curled in my chest, but I swallowed it down. If the Theion would not let me in, then I would call upon the one who always did.

"Zayd."

I spoke his name into the air, turning my head as if he might be there, just out of reach. But the crowd was a sea of strangers, their faces unfamiliar, their gazes slipping past me without pause.

"Zayd!"

People glanced at me now, wary, confused. I pulled my phone from my pocket as if I'd done it a thousand times before, pressed it to my ear, pretending I wasn't shouting into the wind like a madman.

"Zayd."

The air shifted.

Subtle, but unmistakable. A ripple through the fabric of the world, a presence slipping between the seams. I knew it instantly, the way one knows the rhythm of their own heartbeat. A Daimon had stepped into the mortal realm.

But it wasn't Zayd.

It wasn't the storm-eyed immortal I ached for.

A figure emerged, golden-haired, sun-kissed, freckles scattered like constellations across high cheekbones. No wings, but the disguise was paper-thin. He still wore the garments of his kind—soft, flowing white, an echo of what he was.

An Eudaimon.

It was not the face I longed for, but it was familiar—friendly, even. "Arestis," I said, lowering the phone.

His hazel eyes went wide, his steps careful, measured as his hands clasped in front of him. "Eryx." My name came from his lips like a question, not a statement.

People were staring. He noticed. He tucked a loose strand of hair behind his ear, flashing a harmless smile, offering an easy lie. "Drama department. Costume fitting."

A few heads turned away, placated.

I arched a brow. "Really?"

"It worked," he muttered. Then, quieter, "What is going on here?"

I almost laughed. "You tell me."

Arestis let out a breath, eyes darting around before finally settling on mine. "This is... not how this was supposed to go." He smiled, but there was no humor in it. Only something tight, something strained.

"Eryx, I need you to go back to sleep."

I blinked. "Huh?"

"Just a little nap. That's all. Say for half a century?"

His voice was calm, gentle. His fingertip tapped against my nose, light as a whisper.

"Half a...?" My limbs went heavy. My vision blurred. "Wait—you can't just—do..."

Darkness swallowed the rest.

I woke with a sharp inhale, my body lurching upright as if I had been drowning in sleep.

The room was dim, illuminated with a dull lamplight, the edges of it blurred with the remnants of a dream I couldn't hold onto. My head still ached, a dull, insistent throb, but before I could dwell on it, movement caught my eye.

Arestis paced at the foot of the bed, fingers fidgeting at his sides, his wings stiff and ruffled—pale as snowfall, dusted with darker flecks along the edges, every feather quivering with tension. He was mumbling under his breath, words too soft to catch.

I moved without thinking, closing the distance between us in two steps. My hand found the front of his robe, fisting the fabric, and his heels lifted slightly from the ground as I pulled him toward me.

"Where is Zayd?" My voice came low, steady.

Arestis let out a strangled noise, something between a yelp and a whimper. "Ahh! You were supposed to reset!" His hands scrambled at my wrist, weak in their grip.

"Reset?" My brows drew together. "What the hell are you talking about?"

"The Theion didn't tell me this would happen," he huffed, lip trembling in something like frustration, or perhaps fear. "Maybe I did something wrong. ...Oh, Theion, will they forgive me for what I did unknowingly?" His hazel eyes grew wet, his mouth forming a slight pout. "Why was I the one forced to watch over your first reincarnation?"

"My first what?"

He groaned, tilting his head back with theatrical misery. "If you're going to hurt me, just make it quick." He raised a hand to his forehead like a tragic heroine, breath shuddering. "It's pathetic enough to be manhandled by a mortal—"

By a mortal?

I let him go.

He stumbled but recovered quickly, adjusting his robes with forced dignity. "Take a seat, uh—Eryx." He gestured toward the bed.

Now that I was paying attention, I realized—I knew this room.

And yet, I didn't.

The walls were cluttered with posters, bands and sports teams, their colors faded with time. Trophies lined the shelves, interspersed with photographs—smiling faces frozen in youth, arms slung around each other in familiarity. My friends. My life.

Me.

A child's room, stretched thin into adulthood.

Memories unfurled like ink spilling across parchment, soaking into the edges of my mind. This room—this small, familiar space—had been filled with warmth once. A mother's hands pulling the blankets up to my chin, a father's playful indifference as he pretended not to see the small feet poking out from beneath the bed. Laughter had lived here. So had boredom. So had the quiet, steady hum of a life unfolding.

But sorrow crept in, thick and cloying, bleeding into the recollections until they were no longer just memories but wounds. Doubt settled in my bones, expectation pressed heavy on my chest, and loneliness wrapped itself around me like a second skin. And then, beneath it all, there was loss—deep, hollowing, an ache so profound it caught in my throat and refused to let go.

A cold weight settled in my stomach. "Where is Zayd?" I asked again.

Arestis hesitated, lifting a hand as if to stall me, his lips parting—then shutting. His throat bobbed as he swallowed. "Promise you'll listen to everything I have to say before you get... heated?" He exhaled. "Zayd is... dead."

I stilled.

He flinched. "It—it was a year ago. A year ago today, actually. Odd, isn't it?" His fingers tapped against his chin as if this were some minor puzzle, his brows drawing together in thought.

I barely heard him.

"What do you mean?" The words scraped from my throat, raw and disbelieving. A joke. A fever dream. It had to be.

"Daimons can't die," I said, firmer this time, daring him to challenge it.

His expression softened. "Zayd was human."

Arestis stepped closer, voice quieter now. "Eryx... where do you think you are? *When* do you think you are?"

I had no answer. I could only stare.

"You remember, don't you? Giving yourself to Erebos. Sacrificing your immortality—for a mortal's."

The memory surged, sudden and violent. Blood on concrete. Silas, dying. Zayd, pleading. The Theion's silence. The mists swallowing me whole.

And his smile. That beautiful, infuriating, beloved smile.

I closed my eyes against the onslaught, swallowing hard.

"Zayd was punished for bringing a mortal into Khaos," Arestis continued. "Stripped of his immortality. Made human. He lived out his life alongside Philetos." A pause. "Eryx... you became a part of Erebos sixty years ago."

I opened my eyes.

"The Theion decided to restart your cycle," he said. "Kasius—" He gestured at me. "He is your first reincarnation."

A sharp laugh forced itself from my throat. "And yet, he... we remember everything?"

He sighed. "That... shouldn't be possible."

It was too much. Too much all at once. I had given up everything because I refused to live in a world without Zayd. And in some cruel twist of fate—that's exactly what had happened.

A gentle knock at the door cut through the silence.

Arestis gasped, his entire body jolting as he turned, then—vanished.

"Kas?" A voice, soft and hesitant. "Are you okay? I heard yelling."

I knew that voice. An unfamiliar warmth bloomed in my chest, gentle yet unwavering. Comfort. Acceptance. Not the fleeting kind offered out of obligation, but something deeper.

Mother.

"I'm fine," I said, the response slipping from my lips before I even processed it. "Just a... phone call with a friend."

I listened to her footsteps retreat down the hall before sinking onto the bed, staring up at a ceiling dotted with glow-in-the-dark stars.

A dry, humorless chuckle escaped me.

"So he finally got to watch Philetos grow old." My voice was barely above a whisper. "And now I'm stuck here. In the body of a fuckboy college kid still living with his mother."

I exhaled sharply, rolling onto my side, pressing my face into the pillow.

I washed my face in the library's bathroom, letting the cold water linger on my skin a little longer than necessary. It grounded me, anchored me in this body that wasn't mine but was, in a city that wasn't unfamiliar but felt entirely fucked up.

Los Angeles. *Again.* The same city I technically died in.

Kasius.

That was my name now. Or rather, the name of the body I was wearing.

I dragged my fingers through dark brown hair, slicking it with water, before tracing the sharp lines of my jaw, the angles unfamiliar yet worn into me now like a well-loved path. My gaze drifted lower, catching on the ink curling along the side of my neck, winding down to my shoulder—a dark serpent coiled in quiet repose. I huffed out a laugh. In the form I once chose, I bore something eerily similar. A different time, a different body, yet here it was again.

I rolled my shoulders, exhaling. I missed it—the freedom of shifting, of slipping between faces like water between fingers. But I supposed the one staring back at me was handsome enough. Would've been a shame if it wasn't, given the on-paper credentials.

Prom King. High school football star. Turned down a scholarship. Took a two-year gap, then shuffled his way back to the University of Southern California, slogging through a Sports Science degree. One year left, and then two more for his MAT. Seems he wanted to work with athletes rather than be one. Sensible, I supposed. Less pressure, fewer concussions.

Depression. Anxiety. An impressive history of whoring around and drinking.

I sighed, flicking at the hem of my plain t-shirt beneath my dark flannel. Needs a wardrobe update too.

Tilting my head back, I squinted at the flickering fluorescent light above me. "Just send my consciousness back to Erebos, please."

The only sound was a buzzing from the light.

"Figures."

I stepped out of the bathroom, the wooden door swinging shut behind me as I made my way to the front desk. The library was bathed in the last light of the setting sun, gold bleeding through the dust-heavy air, catching the faint movement of floating particles.

At the desk, an older librarian was unloading books from a cart, stacking them with practiced efficiency. Her glasses had slipped down to the tip of her nose, deep lines carving shadows beneath her eyes.

"Excuse me," I said, leaning against the counter. "Where do you keep your archives?"

She glanced up, adjusting her glasses with a slow blink. "Back section, far left, past the biographies. Most materials are free access for learning and research. If there's something you can't find, let me know—we may need to schedule an appointment." More books thudded onto the desk. "Most records are available digitally. I can help you with that?"

"No, thanks." I smiled, easy and effortless. "I prefer physical materials."

She gave a small nod, already turning back to her work.

I tapped the desk lightly in thanks and wandered toward the archive section. The library was quiet—well, of course it was, it was a library—but even for its closing hour, it held that particular hush, the kind that felt reverent, expectant.

A few students sat at scattered tables, furiously typing, trying to squeeze in just a little more work before the doors locked for the night. A couple of librarians moved through the aisles, shelving books, tidying up, treading softly as if careful not to disturb the walls themselves.

The archive section was tucked away in the back, a long row of shelves filled with bound newspapers, historical records, and aging, yellowed pages carrying the weight of lost time. The scent of ink and old paper clung to the air—faint but unmistakable.

It was mostly empty, save for one other person.

A man sat at the far end, hunched over a table, fingers threading absently through his black hair as he pored over a spread of newspaper articles. He was so absorbed that he hadn't even noticed me enter. A rare sight. Most people had an awareness, that strange prickle at the back of their necks when someone new entered a space.

I let my gaze drift over him, curiosity tugging at me, before turning to the shelves.

I needed obituaries.

One year ago today.

My fingers trailed over the spines of the bound newspapers, the rough texture grounding me, keeping me from thinking too much. Too much about Zayd. About the power I had given up. About the future I had stumbled into taking control of.

Let's see what the world had to say about the day Zayd died.

There was nothing.

I exhaled, pulling a different volume from the shelf, and flipped it open.

No Zayd, no Silas. No Vassallo.

Surely, they were cheesy enough to die around the same time—one of them from a broken heart, or both of them holding hands, whispering final words as they took their last breath together.

The thought made me chuckle under my breath, the sound slipping out before I could process the implications of it. Across from me, the stranger lifted his head, dark eyes peering over his glasses, then returned to his papers without a word.

Great. Now I was the guy laughing at obituaries.

Maybe Arestis got the day wrong. I flipped through the other volumes, scanning the dates before and after. Nothing.

With a sigh I let my gaze drift toward my archive companion's papers. Just a glance, a peek—old habits died hard, and curiosity had always been my favorite vice.

The names struck me first. Rossi, Ivanov, Chang, Callaghan... *Legare.*

Ah. Interesting.

And then, names I didn't recognize. New players, perhaps. The stranger was combing through a century's worth of Los Angeles's filth, meticulously piecing together the lineage of its corrupt elite. I knew those names well—how delicious their desires, how predictable their ambitions. Mortals never changed.

I stepped closer and leaned in, chest brushing his shoulder as I spotted the article I needed. "Sorry, I need this," I murmured, fingers curling around the page.

A hand shot out, gripping the other end.

"Excuse me?" He yanked back.

"I said please."

"No, you didn't." His grip held firm, gaze locking onto mine. Stormy dark gray eyes, sharp and unreadable.

"Pretty sure I did." I gave a single, decisive tug and lifted the paper high, turning away as I scanned the pages with ease.

Behind me, a chair scraped against the floor. "What is your problem?"

I ignored him. My breath hitched as I found it—the black-and-white portrait of Zayd and Silas. One from their wedding day, and another, more recent, from the same year they died.

My expression softened.

They had passed on the same day. Together. Peacefully in bed. Of course they did. And now they had a quiet eternity in Erebos, reliving the best of their years, wrapped in the warmth of something even gods had failed to tear apart.

A voice cut through my thoughts. "Are you—are you okay?"

I blinked. Wetness clung to my lashes, streaked my cheeks.

Tears.

I had not cried since the day I died.

"Fuck," I muttered, swiping a hand over my face. "Yeah. Here." Without meeting his gaze, I held the paper out to him.

He hesitated. Then, carefully, "Did you know the Vassallos?"

"Just old friends."

"Friends with seventy-year-olds?" His brow arched. "What are you, like, twenty?"

I scoffed. "I am older than your entire bloodline, mort—" I bit my tongue, adjusting. "Twenty-three. *Thank you very much.*"

I moved toward his table, casting an idle glance over the mess of documents, notes scribbled in the margins, articles carefully taken out and stacked. All organized crime.

"What's all this?"

"None of your business." He hastily gathered the papers, placing a notebook over them as if that could erase my already-forming suspicions.

Before I could press further, a sharp clearing of a throat made us both look up.

A librarian stood at the edge of the aisle, arms crossed. "Gentlemen, it's time for you two to leave. We've had complaints about the noise."

My new friend glanced at the stack of papers. Then at the librarian.

Oh. *You little shit.*

I recognized that look—contemplation, calculation, the flickering thought of theft crossing his mind. *How cute.*

I shifted forward, lowering my voice to something pathetic and pleading. "Ma'am, wait—can you help me find my sister real quick? She said she'd be in the romance section, and if I leave without her, my parents will kill me."

She sighed, already turning. "Make it quick."

I followed for a few steps, then flicked a glance over my shoulder. Sure enough, he was slipping the documents into his bag, heading briskly for the exit.

I smirked. "Actually," I called out, rubbing the back of my neck sheepishly. "I forgot—my sister's at home."

The librarian turned, unimpressed.

"Have a good night!" I shot her a quick grin and strolled toward the door.

I spotted him half a block down, walking fast, head down, the kind of pace that screamed I definitely didn't just steal something from a public institution.

Then came a car.

Sleek, black, expensive. It pulled up too fast, too sharply. He stopped short, nearly tripping over himself, and took a hasty step back. *That's probably not his ride.* My own steps quickened, closing the distance just as the doors swung open.

Two men stepped out. Suits crisp, shoes polished, the weight of wealth and violence draped over them like second skins. The kind of men whose pockets were lined with blood money, who had long since stopped wondering whether their souls could be saved.

"Aw," the thief tilted his head, voice light, taunting. "Is your boss's ego really that fragile? Must match that little—"

He never finished. Because the moment he took another step back, he hit my chest.

"Do we have a problem here, gentlemen?" I slung an arm around his shoulders, flashing them a bright, easy grin.

They turned to me, slow, measured. Eyes cold. Empty.

Theions, how familiar this feels.

"Get lost, kid," one of them said, voice like gravel.

The other took a step forward, adjusting his jacket just enough for me to catch the gleam of metal beneath the fabric. "We've come to send a message."

"Naturally," the thief cut in, glib and careless, as if he weren't about to get a large hospital bill and a referral to a plastic surgeon.

Then the ugly one raised a fist.

And like an absolute idiot, I stepped in the way.

Pain.

Pain.

A sharp, splintering sensation exploded across my nose. Stars burst behind my eyes. Fuck, I forgot what pain felt like. Was it supposed to feel this sharp? This immediate? My breath hitched, the dull throb settling in. Shit. It might actually be broken.

I shook my head, blinking through the sting. And then, because I am a dumbass, I did the only thing I could—I punched him back. My fist met his face, and a second, sharper pain shot up my arm.

"Fuck," I hissed, shaking my knuckles out. "That hurt just as much."

The man I hit stumbled back, stunned, more out of surprise than actual damage.

His friend grabbed at the collar of my shirt. "Who the fuck are you?"

I opened my mouth. "I'm his—" But when I glanced sideways, that little shit was already gone—leaving me here to eat fists on his behalf.

I stared at them. They stared at me.

"Bye," I said simply, shaking out of his grip and booking it. Thank the Theion that Kasius was at least young and athletic.

CHAPTER TWO

"Well, that was spectacularly stupid." Arestis sighed, pressing a cotton ball soaked in antiseptic against the bridge of my nose. The sting flared, sharp and immediate, and I winced. "You have to be careful in this form," he added, dabbing at the bruise like a disappointed nursemaid.

I huffed, tilting my head back against the headboard. "How was I supposed to know I'd get clocked in the face? I didn't even plan to do this tonight. I just wanted..."

The words trailed off. *What did I want?*

"I know. I followed you."

Unspoken things stretched between us. The weight of centuries, the echo of choices made. Since the day I had found Zayd in Khaos, impaled by the Theion's judgment, writhing through the endless cycle of his suffering, he had been my fixation. My curiosity. My endless amusement—until he wasn't. Until he became something else. Something I could not name then, and perhaps could not name now.

Humans were supposed to be simple creatures. Fickle, fleeting, disposable. And yet, this body—this mind—proved otherwise. The emotions roiling beneath my skin were more than relics of a past life; they were deeper, sharper, pulling me toward something I did not understand but yet I yearned for.

But next to that yearning, something else stirred. Not anger—I could never be angry with Zayd—but a quiet, aching weight...

Arestis straightened, snapping the first aid kit shut and placing it on Kasius' desk. "Just make sure you're taking care of this life, Eryx. A human life is a fragile thing. Take advantage of being able to live. Embrace it. Not many Daimon get this opportunity—to go back. To..."

He didn't finish the thought, and he didn't need to. He would never say it aloud, never give voice to the heresy that sat heavy between us. But we had all wondered, at one point or another. Watching mortals from the fringes, watching them stumble and grieve and love, we had all, at least once, ached to know what it felt like to *be*.

And now I had it. A body that actually breathed. A heart that actually beat. A life that could be lived. I should have been grateful. Instead, I was alone.

The realization sat bitter on my tongue, something I had refused to name until now. I was nothing without *him*. He had become my purpose. I exhaled sharply, shaking my head as if I could shake off the thoughts with it.

What is with this talk? These feelings?

"Does this mean you're not going to find a way to send me back?" I asked instead, voice lighter but not enough to hide the uncertainty beneath. "I shouldn't be here. It's not fair to Kasius."

Arestis met my gaze, steady. "It's not as though you swapped places. He isn't lying dormant somewhere inside you or in Erebos. You just... remember." He hesitated, then continued, voice gentler. "It's a messy thing, I know. But you don't need to bear guilt for a life you haven't stolen. Philetos went through the same process."

I flinched at the name.

"All mortals carry echoes of their past selves," he went on. "Fragments of old lives, old habits, old loves. Once, they could even reach back into their past wisdoms, but those practices have been long forgotten." He stepped forward, pressing a firm finger to my chest. "You are Kasius. And he is you. Live as he would. Follow his path and you will see."

I gazed up at him, lips thinning. "This is why Kakodai never hang out with you feathered softies," I muttered, but the words lacked their usual bite. He would know what I meant. He would know that, beneath it, there was gratitude.

Arestis only smiled, stepping back. "Rest now. You have classes in the morning."

I groaned. "Do I have to?"

"There are great things in store for you, Kas. That is why you have an Eudai, after all."

I snorted. "I thought you said you were forced to be my guide?"

He winked, the gesture infuriatingly carefree. "Details."

And then he was gone.

I let out a breath, long and slow, as I stood before the heavy wooden doors of the lecture hall. *Advanced Physiology*, the plaque read.

Ridiculous.

I had watched cities rise from dust and fall back into it, had seen empires crumble beneath their own ambition, witnessed wars waged over love and land and things far pettier. I had stood at the edge of plagues, watching as the divine weighed lives like stones in a hand. And yet—this. This was where I found myself. Trapped in a mortal body, forced into the monotony of academia.

I pushed open the door, slipping inside with the ease of routine. My feet carried me to my usual seat, tucked just far enough back that the professor struggled to see past the rows of heads in front of me. A strategic choice. The less Kas was noticed, the less he was called on. The less we were called on, the less we had to disappoint—or worse, entertain. Because that was the expectation, wasn't it? The charming, careless athlete, throwing out jokes to mask how little he actually knew.

And I had always played my part well.

I sprawled into my chair, flipping my notebook open as my chin came to rest against my palm. Half-listening, half-doodling, letting the words of the lecture drift over me like background noise.

At first.

But then—

A phrase caught me, unexpected. Something about cellular adaptation, about how muscles tear only to rebuild stronger, about the body's ceaseless effort to refine itself through stress and struggle.

My fingers twitched, pen poised above paper.

The autonomic response to exertion triggers a cascade of biochemical adaptations—

The cardiovascular system recalibrates, optimizing oxygen transport—

The words sank in, something in my mind latching onto them with an almost feral hunger. The science of movement, of strain, of how far the human body could be pushed before it broke. And more importantly—how it healed. How it overcame.

Fascinating.

My pen began to move. Scrawling notes, underlining key terms, my own thoughts filling the margins. Not just copying—understanding. Absorbing. This was learning. This was something beyond memorization, beyond routine plays and reflexive action. Anyone could be taught how to throw a ball, how to run a route, how to win a game. But this—this was knowing why. The mechanics of it, the way the body responded and fought to improve itself. It was survival, but more than that—it was ascendancy.

A slow grin pulled at my lips.

I had watched the divine mold the world with a flick of their hands. And yet here was proof of something just as miraculous—human bodies, human minds, reshaping themselves through nothing but their own sheer will.

"Class dismissed."

The professor's voice shattered the moment, his book snapping shut atop the podium. The rustle of students packing up filled the hall, and I leaned back in my chair, feeling the distinct and unexpected pang of... disappointment?

Already?

I exhaled, stretching my arms overhead as boredom curled at the edges of my thoughts once more. Who would've guessed—being forced to sit still and learn could actually be fun.

And then the thought hit me.

I was a fucking nerd in a nice body.

I blinked, staring down at my own notes—neatly written, underlined, annotated in the margins like I actually cared—and felt something cold and startling settle in my chest.

I had underestimated you. Kasius. I mean me. Us.

I rubbed a hand over my face. This was getting complicated and confusing.

Classes passed in a blur, sliding into place as if they had always belonged to me. I didn't stumble, didn't fumble—just fell into step with the rhythm of Kasius' life as though I had been living it all along. I avoided conversation where I could, kept my head down, let the excuse of a hangover do the work for me when people asked why I was quieter than usual. They all accepted it without question, nodding in understanding, as if I were some tragic soldier in the eternal war of college debauchery.

By the time I threw my backpack into the backseat of my car, the itch had settled deep in my bones. The Vassallo estate. Was it still standing? Had time gutted the place? It wasn't far. It was a Friday, and from what I had gathered, this guy's weekends consisted of studying, drinking and fucking, so I figured a quick road trip wouldn't disrupt the routine too much.

The iron gates stood open when I arrived, black metal yawning wide as if welcoming me to a piece of the past. Above them, a sign I didn't recognize was welded into the arch, the letters gleaming in the late afternoon sun. They had donated the estate when they died. *Of course they did.* An art charity, for medically fragile youth, adults, seniors—those tangled in the inescapable web of mental illness, of social struggles. I let out a breath of laughter, quiet and wry, before driving through the gates.

Inside, I picked up a brochure, flipping through its pages with idle fingers. It documented the estate's history, the artwork donated by its previous owners, and the charity's mission. Nowhere did it mention that this had once been the beating heart of one of LA's most powerful Italian crime families. That these halls had once been ruled by Legare. I walked slowly, the sound of my footsteps echoing as my eyes roved the paintings, not truly seeing them. I thought of Zayd and Silas, of how they must have spent their days here. Had Legare truly died with them? Or had it begun to wither long before they ever set foot in Erebos?

And then—there. A familiar face, scowling in concentration at a painting, dark brows pulled together as he studied it with far too much intensity. A brochure clutched in his hand, forgotten in his over-analysis.

My little archive thief.

"Well, look who we have here," I purred, stepping behind him, leaning in just close enough that my breath ghosted against his ear.

He stiffened, exhaling a quiet, "Shit."

I reached out, fingers curling around his arm just as he tried to step away. "Not so fast. You wouldn't dare abandon me again, would you, thief?"

His eyes flicked around the room, scanning for eavesdroppers. "Keep your voice down," he hissed. "You can't just throw accusations like that around in a place like this."

"Who were those guys?" I asked, tilting my head. "Why did you steal from the library? Do you realize how dangerous it is to be researching those names?"

"One question at a time, big guy." He adjusted his glasses. "How about you let go of me, and we discuss this somewhere more private?"

I let go.

And the little shit ran.

I cursed under my breath, lunging after him, my voice ringing through the corridor with theatrical ease.

"Help! That man is stealing something—uh, something valuable! Art thief!"

His head whipped around, eyes wide with disbelief as he shouted, "Are you kidding me?"

I grinned and ran faster. Following him out of the manor, steps unhurried as he rushed ahead, nearly tripping over himself in his desperation to escape. He made a beeline for a small electric car, yanking open the driver's side door with shaking hands. Before he could slam it shut, I slid into the passenger seat, the doors clicking closed in near unison.

"What are you doing?" he barked, breathless, his brows pulled tight in disbelief. "Get out!"

I smiled, slow and deliberate, as I reached over and pressed the lock down on my side. "You said you'd answer my questions if we went somewhere private."

His dark eyes swept over my face, narrowing as they landed on my nose. Damn. The makeup must have started to fade, revealing the bruising beneath.

"Are you crazy?" His voice was lower now, taut with something between suspicion and alarm.

I tilted my head, feigning thoughtfulness. "I took a punch to the face for *you*. And I gave *you* the opening to steal those documents. *You* owe me."

He stared, utterly dumbfounded by my audacity. But before he could retort, another car pulled into the estate's drive, rolling to a stop. A police car. Two officers stepped out, climbing the stairs toward the entrance.

I flicked my gaze back to him, watching the way his body went rigid. His fingers twitched toward the controls. With a slow, almost lazy movement, I pulled up the lock on my side.

He pressed the button immediately, locking it again.

"What's wrong, little thief?" I murmured, voice laced with amusement. "I thought you wanted me to leave."

His jaw tightened. "Buckle up, asshole."

The car lurched into motion, peeling out of the lot, leaving my car and the cops behind.

I watched the estate shrink in the distance before turning back to him. "My name is Jaehyun, by the way," he muttered under his breath. "Not thief."

"Jaehyun," I repeated, rolling the syllables over my tongue. "I'm Kas." The name tumbled out before I could stop it. "Kasius Nikolaou."

His hands flexed on the wheel. "Hm." A pause. His eyes stayed on the road, but I could see his thoughts turning. "Well, Kasius—why is it that you were at the library yesterday looking into the Vassallos, and then today you're skulking around their old estate? Did you actually know them, or is this some weird game where you're just stalking me?"

His foot pressed heavier on the gas.

"Whoa, buddy, slow down," I said, finally reaching for my seatbelt.

The speedometer climbed higher.

Shit. I straightened in my seat, pulse kicking up. "I'm not following you, okay? Silas was my—what—third cousin? I was doing a paper on family history. Something about, uh—how habits run in families and affect physiological responses to exercise." I waved a hand vaguely. "That's it! I swear!"

He let out a short breath, but the car didn't slow.

"Look, man, I'm just trying to graduate, alright? I needed a subject. Turns out my family history is more interesting than I thought. That's all."

Jaehyun's grip on the wheel eased, his foot lifting slightly off the pedal. The car began to decelerate.

"You're related to the Vassallos?" he muttered, as if testing the words in his mouth. "How much do you know about your family? Do you know about Legare?"

I exhaled sharply. "I answered your question. Now it's your turn." I turned to him, voice firm. "Who were those guys at the library? And what exactly are you looking for?"

"My name is Jaehyun Seok. I'm a journalist at GCG."

GCG. The Golden Coast Gazette. So that was it. This reckless little human was writing a piece on LA's crime syndicates. No wonder there was a target on his back.

I let out a low whistle, leaning back against the seat. "That explains your seedy friends." I turned my head slightly, studying him. He had one of those faces—delicate but sharp, all soft lines and dark, intelligent eyes. The kind of face that would've bruised beautifully if those bastards had gotten their hands on him.

"You look young," I mused. "Are you a rookie? That would explain why you picked such a risky and dumb topic for an article."

He didn't even blink. "I'm thirty-two."

I snorted. "Right."

His fingers tightened around the wheel.

"Why don't you pick a safer topic?" I continued, feigning casual interest. "You'll get to keep that pretty face intact and, you know, expand your life expectancy."

"You really think those reasons will stop me? Do I look like a quitter?"

His gaze flicked to mine, and for a moment, something in my chest tightened. A flash of something, a fond memory. He reminded me of *him*. Beautiful softness with dark features, and an annoyingly stubborn personality. Heat crept up my neck. What were these feelings? I turned away, fixing my eyes on the passing streets. "Where are we going?"

"I don't know," he muttered, adjusting his glasses before gripping the wheel again. "I think I'm detaining you for questioning."

I huffed out a laugh. "Detaining me? You're not a cop. Reporters can't do that."

He ignored me.

"Have you heard of the Iron Bratva?"

The name sent something skittering through my mind. A thread of recognition, buried deep.

Jaehyun must've caught the flicker of reaction on my face, because he pressed on. "Those guys that came after me. They're part of the Russian mafia. A branch off Ivanov."

I felt my brows lift, despite myself. *Ivanov.* Now that was a name I definitely knew.

Jaehyun's eyes sharpened. "Interesting," he murmured, more to himself than to me.

He took a sharp turn, the kind that sent my shoulder slamming into the door. The seatbelt bit into my chest, and I let out a strangled sound that I would later deny was anything close to a yelp.

"Can I be let out, please?" My voice cracked, undignified.

"We're being followed. I can't stop." His knuckles were white against the wheel, his jaw set like stone.

"*We're* not being followed," I said, rolling my head to look at him. "*You* are."

"And you, by association."

"You know, there's this great service called the police? Maybe you've heard of them?"

Jaehyun scoffed, shooting me a quick, incredulous look. "You know about the mafia and don't know that sometimes they are the police?" His voice was dry, but beneath it, something sharp and bitter. He wove through traffic with a reckless sort of precision, like he'd done this before.

I didn't answer right away. He had a point. The mafia wasn't just criminals playing at kings; they had roots in every crack of society. Cops, politicians, doctors, lawyers—the whole damn tree was rotten.

I sighed, raking a hand through my hair. "How deep are you in this mess?"

"Given that I'm a journalist, my identity isn't exactly a secret, and that we've been tailed since we left the estate?" His fingers tightened around the wheel. "I'd say balls deep."

A laugh slipped from me, light and unbothered despite the knot tightening in my gut. "I can help you get out of this. Get them to lay off." The words came without thought, but the moment I said them, they felt like an inevitability. Maybe there was a reason I woke up in this body, in this moment. Maybe this meeting was more than chance. "I know more about Ivanov than you might assume."

Jaehyun's grip didn't loosen. His eyes stayed fixed ahead, sharp and calculating. "I don't want them to lay off." His voice was quiet, but there was steel beneath it. "I want them to crumble."

"Really?" My laughter faltered. A slow, deliberate blink as I realized he was serious. "You're just one human. How exactly do you plan to pull that off?"

"I'm going to kill the head."

The air between us shifted, something colder curling at the edges. I searched his face, still waiting for the punchline. It never came. "That's murder," I said slowly. "How do you expect to get away with it while writing an expose on them?"

Jaehyun's lips twitched, but it wasn't a smile. "I never said I was writing an expose."

I frowned. "You said you were researching them because you're a journalist."

"I never said that I was writing an expose though." He flicked his gaze toward me, dark and unreadable. "You just assumed."

Silence stretched between us, taut and unspoken.

Then, he exhaled, his shoulders easing just slightly. "I think I lost them." He slowed the car, the tension in the air thinning.

I should get out now. Walk away. Keep Kas safe. Jaehyun clearly had a death wish, and I'd lived through enough centuries to recognize when someone was chasing their own ruin.

And yet—

There was something about him, something in the way his recklessness felt familiar and comforting.

The thought barely had time to settle before the world jolted.

A flash of headlights. The blare of horns. Tires screaming against pavement.

Then—impact.

The world tilted, my skull rattling as everything spun. Sound warped, fading in and out like we were underwater. My fingers twitched, grasping at nothing.

"Kas," Jaehyun's voice reached me, muffled and distant.

A blinding light. Shadows moving.

"He's stable." A voice I didn't recognize.

Then—nothing.

This feeling was familiar.

The sluggish weight of my limbs, the slow drag of consciousness clawing its way back. My head throbbed with a dull insistent ache. But this time I didn't awake to perfumed sheets or a naked woman's body draped over mine. Instead, the sterile scent of antiseptic burned my nose, the steady beep of a heart monitor filled the silence, and the harsh glow of fluorescent lights pried my eyes open.

I groaned, shifting against the hospital bed's too-thin mattress. A scrape of metal against metal caught my attention, the rattling hooks of a curtain being pulled aside. Jaehyun stood there, a hospital gown draped over his frame, one hand gripping the IV pole like it was a scepter. His dark eyes found mine, assessing.

"I told them it was an accident," he said.

"Lying comes so naturally to you, doesn't it?" My voice was hoarse, dry as parchment.

"Clearly. I'm a journalist."

My fingers drifted up, finding the small bandages dotting my face, the faint sting of scrapes beneath them.

"Just a mild concussion. Some cuts from the glass. No major damage, pretty boy." He sat on the edge of my bed, the weight of him barely shifting the mattress. Silence stretched between us, thick with unspoken things.

Then—"What are you thinking about? Are you going to talk to the police?"

I exhaled slowly, my fingers tracing absent patterns over the IV line in my arm. The skin there was bruised, a sickly bloom of purple and yellow. "I'm just trying to figure out what the fuck your plan is. How long until they stop playing and come for you in earnest? And when they do, how long until they kill you?" I glanced at him. "But that just leaves me with more questions."

Jaehyun tilted his head, studying me. "Ask them, then."

"So you are a journalist, but you're not writing a piece on... them." I kept my voice low. Hospitals had ears, and I had no illusions about who might be listening. "Then why are they sending people after you? What did you do? And what did they do to make you want their downfall? Did they kill your parents? Your dog?"

Something flickered in his gaze. Not anger, not grief—something deeper, buried too far down to name.

"I'll tell you," he said. "If you tell me everything you know about them." A smirk, sharp at the edges. "Call it strangers with benefits. I tell you, you tell me."

"You're that desperate?" I arched a brow. "Trusting a stranger not to fuck you over? Weren't you worried earlier that I was working with them or at least a creepy stalker?"

"I did my homework while you were out." He leaned back slightly, like a cat pleased with itself. "Slipped your wallet from your belongings when the nurses brought it in. Background check. Kasius Nikolaou, twenty-three, junior at USC. Father—Alexander Nikolaou, deceased. Smoke inhalation while providing emergency services to a complex fire. Mother—Lela Nikolaou, nurse at this very hospital. Alive, but drowning in debt to put her son through college because he declined a scholarship to fuck around. Though, we all know it's because you couldn't cope with your father's death."

The words cut like a blade slipped between ribs, quiet and precise. My hands curled into fists, knuckles white against the sheets.

Jaehyun's voice remained even. "So, to answer the question you were alluding to—no, I'm not worried you'll fuck me over, or that you're working with them. Quite the opposite." A pause, a considering look. "I don't know how someone like you would have information I don't, but color me intrigued. And, I suppose, a little desperate."

His tone was deadpan, like he hadn't just laid me bare and wiped his boots on the remains.

"What's wrong? Did I hurt your feelings, kid?"

I swallowed down the heat rising in my throat, forcing my hands to relax. *Remember yourself, Eryx.*

"No." I met his gaze, calm, steady. "Clearly your background check could only go so far." A deliberate beat. "Those two years I took off from school? I spent them in the very world you're trying to dismantle." A lie, but laced with enough truth to feel real. "I know who operates what, who owns who. The contracts, the agreements, the pressure points that could bring them down—or prop them up."

A bold claim. I saw it in his eyes, the sharp gleam of calculation. He knew it too. But the thing was—I did know all of it. Just sixty years too late. The landscape had shifted, names and faces changed. But I knew someone who could fill in the gaps.

Jaehyun pushed off my bed, steadying himself against his IV pole. He studied me for a long moment, then gave a short nod.

"Strangers with benefits it is, then."

I scoffed. "I don't see what my benefits are."

"I'm a journalist at the last independent outlet in LA. We always pay our anonymous sources handsomely." His gaze flicked to me, assessing. "Let me interview you. Help your mother pay for that tuition." He turned, heading for his own bed. "And then we're done. Back to strangers."

But that was the problem. I wasn't anonymous anymore. My face had been seen with his—more than once. When he makes his move, when he fails, they will kill him. And then, they would come for me, and possibly my mother.

Either he was a selfish bastard who didn't care that a naive college kid would end up as collateral damage in his crusade, or he was reckless enough to believe he could actually pull this off.

End Ivanov. End the Iron Bratva.

CHAPTER THREE

"Hm, do you think maybe you have a savior complex?" Arestis mused, crossing his legs as he perched at my desk, the chair angled toward me.

I stretched out on my bed, arms folded behind my head. "I wouldn't put it like that."

"Then why do you feel the need to go through with this?" He tapped a lazy finger against the chair's armrest. "He's just a stranger. You are no longer a Daimon. You do not need to intervene."

I let out a slow breath, tracing invisible patterns against the ceiling with my eyes. Sunlight pooled through the window, catching on the star stickers scattered across the surface. In the dark, they shone like constellations. Now, bathed in daylight, they were a sickly, fading green.

"I just..." I began, "Feel like there's a reason I was brought back here. You don't find it odd that I ran into someone connected to—"

"To Zayd," Arestis cut in, his voice tilting downward, that gentle yet insistent tone of someone leading a child toward an obvious conclusion.

I turned my head to look at him, expression dropping. "I was going to say Ivanov."

I had spent centuries as a Kakodaimon, wading through the filth of the powerful, watching as greed rotted men from the inside out. And yet, for every bloated tyrant, there were those who rose against them. The rebellion. The reckoning. The fall. There was a certain poetry to it—watching and aiding empires as they teetered on their pedestals. Watching hands that once held power curl into fists, watching crowns tumble to the dirt. The grand cycle of corruption and collapse. How utterly, endlessly entertaining. Ivanov was just another tyrant, one I used to be all too familiar with.

"Maybe Jaehyun was meant to be my charge," I said, stretching out a leg, the picture of ease. "He seems like my type."

"In more ways than one," Arestis teased.

My skin went hot. I ignored it, but my mind betrayed me, offering up images without permission. Jaehyun's mouth, soft but sharp. The way his lips parted when he was caught off guard. I wondered what he'd look like when stripped of that smug haughtiness—what sounds he'd make when pleasure overtook him.

Shit.

I bent one knee, shifting just enough to mask the hard-on forming in my pants. *Fuck, this body.* I couldn't tell if it was because of his high libido or my own. Either way, it was annoying.

Arestis sighed. "Just be careful, alright? You are—"

"I know." My voice was quieter now. "I'm fragile."

The word tasted bitter. No divinity to shield me, no power to bend the world at my will. Just Kasius. Just human.

"Trust me," I muttered. "I haven't forgotten."

"Well," Arestis said, pushing himself up from the chair. In his hands was a file—thick, stuffed to the brim, edges curling from years of existence. "If we weren't siblings—"

I grimaced, and he caught it immediately, rolling his eyes. "Oh, don't give me that look. You know it's just a phrase."

"Yeah, a phrase that loses meaning when some of us have fucked each other," I muttered.

"If we weren't *friends*," he corrected with an exaggerated sigh, "I wouldn't have done this. You know we aren't supposed to intervene in mortal affairs without permission."

"Eudaimons aren't," I said, leaning back against my pillows. "But Kakodaimons? Free rein. And you, my dear Arestis, are simply working under the whims of a former Kakodaimon. Let that bring you peace of mind." I flashed him a grin.

His expression was flat, unimpressed, but he still placed the file onto the bed beside me. "That law firm you were so interested in? You were right. They had plenty of seedy little documents tucked away, all those names you mentioned. So here you go. Sixty years of history to get you back up to speed."

I hummed, running my fingers along the edges of the stack. There was a weight to it—more than just paper, more than just ink. "I appreciate it," I said, letting my voice soften. "Really, Arestis. I'm glad it's you that's stuck with me."

He exhaled sharply, shaking his head. "I chose to be here."

I tilted my head. "Lying now?"

"What can I say?" He lifted one shoulder, tilting his head in an almost exaggeratedly cute way, nose scrunching slightly. "Kakodaimons are bad influences."

I shook my head, chuckling as he disappeared.

Silence filled the room as I turned my gaze to the documents in front of me. Jaehyun wanted that interview in three days, and thanks to that little car crash, I had a whole week off from classes to "recover." Convenient considering that Arestis healed me.

Now it was time to study up on my old associates and charges.

I stared down at my phone, as a notification chimed. I hadn't wanted to turn it back on, but Jaehyun had insisted—something about needing to coordinate the interview.

My brows pulled together as I read the message he'd sent. An address. Beverly Hills.

K: What is this?

J: The location for our interview. Wear something nice. Formal.

K: What?

J: Just do it.

Almost immediately, two more texts followed.

J: You'd look nice in all black.

J: 6 PM. Meet you at the entrance.

I scoffed, thumb hovering over the keyboard before I gave up and opened my banking app, already knowing the disappointment waiting for me.

And there it was. A tragedy in numbers.

I groaned, flopping back onto the bed. "Fuck... *Arestis.*"

The one good thing about being human—Arestis was my guide. Once a mortal learned their guide's true name, calling them was as simple as breathing, a whisper sent rippling through Khaos like a stone dropped into an endless abyss, calling them to their charge.

Feathers rustled. "Yes, Kasius?" Arestis stood at the foot of my bed, examining his nails as if I had pulled him away from something far more interesting. Which, knowing him, probably not.

"I need another favor," I said, propping myself up on my elbows. "Can we go shopping?"

His expression lifted with amusement. "Like... together?"

"As long as you pay."

Daimons always had their ways—resources, clothes, funds, whatever they desired. The world bent easily to those who had the power to pull its strings.

His lips parted in an exaggerated gasp, a hand pressing to his chest. "Ah, using me. How shocking." But the smile that followed was indulgent. "Fine. Yes, we can."

Before my eyes, his clothing changed—tailored into something more fitting for the time, his wings vanishing as if they had never been there at all. His shoulder-length hair shifted, half-pulled back in a way that framed his face. If I didn't know better, I'd say he looked like some runway model stepping out of a magazine.

He caught me staring and grinned. "I know, I'm pretty. Stop drooling and let's go." The excitement in his voice slipped through despite his best efforts to sound put-upon.

I rolled my eyes, but a smirk pulled at my lips. I knew it wouldn't take much to convince him. Eudaimons were always so bored. Bound by their divine purpose, they watched but never touched, listened but never spoke. In recent times, they weren't even allowed to cross into the mortal realm without permission. Some accepted it, content in their role as silent guardians. But others—others burned with something restless, something close to resentment.

Not just toward the Kakodaimons, who were free to walk among mortals, to whisper in their ears, to shape fate with a careless hand. No, their resentment reached higher—to the Theion themselves.

Of course, they would never act on it.

Well... some did.

My car crawled up the long, looping driveway, its engine a quiet purr against the hum of chatter spilling from the grand entrance ahead. A mansion loomed before me, the kind of place that belonged in glossy architecture magazines—clean-cut modernism with just enough old-money gravitas to make sure no one mistook it for new wealth.

Sleek glass panels framed the towering facade, spilling golden light onto the manicured hedges and marble steps. Sculpted fountains burbled in calculated elegance, their reflections winking in the polished black stone of the circular drive. My car, a modest relic compared to the sleek, imported beasts parked nearby, stuck out like a sore thumb. At least the suit made up for it. The one good thing about rubbing elbows with the elite: they never questioned a well-dressed man.

I handed my keys to the valet, watching as my car was whisked away before another one slid smoothly into place, a well-oiled cycle of excess.

"Kasius."

The voice was unmistakable—measured, smooth, just the right mix of detachment and authority.

Jaehyun stood near the entrance, waiting. His suit, dark gray and tailored within an inch of perfection, skimmed over his frame like it had been made for him alone. The sheen of his watch caught the light, a piece that probably cost more than my medical bill from that ER visit. His shoes, too, screamed money, polished so sharply I could probably see my own stunned expression in them if I looked close enough. He blended in a little too well here.

"What the hell is this?" I asked, gaze flicking to the ornate banners hanging from the entrance: *Securing Tomorrow Together*—a tagline so self-righteous it practically reeked of political ambition.

"Our interview," Jaehyun said, as if that explained anything. He pulled out two lanyards, the laminated badges marked with the word **PRESS** in bold. "Tonight is a fundraiser hosted by Senator Diana Carrington. Raising money for young people wanting to get into cybersecurity and tech." His tone turned dry. "Very noble, very generous, all for the future of the country." Then, his fingers looped the lanyard around my neck, tugging it straight before smoothing the collar of my jacket with quick, practiced motions. "One of her biggest donors is AEGIS Security. And guess who's one of the CEOs of AEGIS?"

He didn't wait for me to answer.

"Nikolai Ivanov. The Iron Bratva. They're posing as Carrington's security team and, on the side, hosting a little... auction." He leaned in slightly, voice dropping low, edged with something sharp. "Illegal weapons, mercenaries, information. The usual shopping list for people who think laws are suggestions."

From what I learned from Jaehyun and the files Arestis retrieved for me, the Iron Bratva is just a branch of Ivanov. Since Legare ended with Silas, Ivanov stepped right up to the throne.

Nikolai Ivanov was heir to one of the most powerful criminal families on the West Coast and the leader of the Iron Bratva. Unlike his father, Dmitriy, who operated in the shadows, Nikolai had learned to balance both worlds. Outwardly, he was a businessman, a tech mogul, a billionaire playboy with a penchant for exclusive nightclubs and tailored suits. Behind closed doors, he was the muscle of the operation, the one who kept their grip tight on the police force, ensuring loyalty through carefully placed bribes and quiet threats. Guns, money laundering, bribery—standard affairs. But recently there had been whispers of human trafficking. A new venture, a new empire rising from the filth of the old one.

Jaehyun's fingers combed through my hair, adjusting strands that had fallen loose. His gaze lingered.

"What?" I asked, tilting my head. "Regretting the all-black suggestion?"

"No..." His eyes traced over me once more before dipping away, voice quieter this time. "Just... you clean up well. Hard to tell you're just some fratty college kid."

I smirked, letting the teasing slip in. "Let me guess—bullied in college? Couldn't make the cut for a fraternity?"

His eyes met mine, steady and unreadable, the kind of cool indifference that made my stomach do something inconvenient. The barest trace of amusement curved at the edge of his mouth, but he didn't take the bait.

"There are a lot of big players here tonight," he said instead, smoothly sidestepping my words. "Time to put that supposed knowledge of yours to the test."

We stepped past security, flashing our badges.

The entrance hall swallowed us in opulence—high, vaulted ceilings dripping with crystal chandeliers, a sea of black-tie guests moving like polished chess pieces across the marble floor. Every surface gleamed, pristine and untouched, a testament to wealth so old it barely needed to flaunt itself. Servers wove between guests, carrying trays of champagne and delicate hors d'oeuvres, their expressions carefully blank.

The banners lined the walls, repeating the senator's empty promise: Securing Tomorrow Together. A convenient lie wrapped in a patriotic bow.

This world was familiar. The polished exteriors, the careful masks, the quiet power plays woven into every glance and handshake. These were the people I had spent my immortality among.

Wealth. Power. Influence.

And beneath it all, rot.

I loved it.

Turns out this brain only worked when it wanted to. Political theater, no matter how grand the staging, was not on its list of interests. I listened—halfheartedly—as the senator wove promises from gilded words, crafting a vision of the future that, like all visions, was designed to be bought. It was always the same. The faces changed, the names rotated, but beneath the rhetoric, the machinery never stopped running: power fed on wealth, and wealth ensured more power.

Jaehyun's voice pulled me back. "Now comes the part where we find out the truth."

The conference hall emptied around us, the flow of bodies shifting toward a smaller, more exclusive room—donors, politicians, media figures, all drawn toward whispered deals and calculated alliances while the conference hall was quietly turned into an auction room for something far less public.

"All of that," Jaehyun continued, "was for show. But here, if you pay attention, you'll see how people actually feel about Carrington and her campaign. Who is aligned with who."

I almost laughed. As if I hadn't spent centuries watching mortals play their games, learning which threads to pull, which obstacles to place, which paths to clear. The difference between words and intent was something I could read as easily as breath fogging up a glass.

I lifted a hand, catching the bartender's attention. "I'm still waiting for that interview, you know."

Jaehyun leaned beside me, arms crossed. "You think drinking will help you pass it?" There was judgment in his tone, cool and amused.

"Hey now, free bar," I said lightly. "Why not take advantage?"

The bartender smiled. "What'll it be?"

I sighed as I felt those judgemental beautiful eyes still on me. "Just water."

Jaehyun hummed approvingly as I took the glass. "Good choice. First question: who holds the most power in this room?"

I took a slow sip, scanning the room with a flicker of amusement. The ones with real power aren't in this room. They were in the shadows, threading their fingers through the system, unseen but ever-present. But I knew he wanted something simpler.

"Tonight?" I murmured, tilting my glass idly. "The power belongs to whoever has the most dirt on everyone else here. Which, by the looks of it..." My gaze settled on a man standing too close to Senator Carrington, their words measured, their glances exchanged with the ease of well-practiced understanding. "That would be Marcus Delgado, Chief of Police."

Jaehyun followed my gaze, his expression unreadable.

"He's the biggest donor here, isn't he?" I continued. "And from what I can see, Carrington and most of her friends—including Ivanov—benefit the most if Delgado keeps his seat. This isn't just about her campaign. It's a display of loyalty. If he stays in power, their secrets stay safe."

I set my glass down with a soft clink. "And secrets," I added, "are the real currency of men like these."

"Good observation," Jaehyun murmured, a flicker of approval softening the sharp lines of his expression. "Now, besides the celebrities padding their charity lists, who are the big players here?"

"Politically or criminally?"

"I thought we agreed the two go hand in hand." He tilted his head slightly, shifting his weight against the counter so that he was facing me fully now, all quiet attention.

A slow smile curled at my lips. I glanced down at my glass, the ice shifting, then took a measured sip. "Politicians have the money and the face, but real power belongs to the ones they pay to do the dirty work. So..." I let my gaze drift over the room, the glittering crowd, the careful theater of it all. Then, I spotted him. "Ah, there's one."

I lifted my glass just slightly in the direction of a man with dark, slicked-back hair, a tattoo peeking from beneath the cuff of his thousand-dollar suit, half-concealed by the glint of a Rolex. "La Mano Ombra. Low-ranking, probably here as a messenger." I let my attention slide past him to Nikolai Ivanov. "And over there—our dear CEO of AEGIS, fashionably late. You'd think he'd have made an appearance sooner—"

My words cut short as I realized he was already looking at me. Not just looking—staring, like he was carving my face into the back of his mind, sharp and unyielding.

I swallowed. "I swear he's staring at me."

Jaehyun didn't even glance his way. His attention, unnervingly, was still on me—dark eyes gleaming beneath the low lights, something unreadable curling at the edges of his lips. "Who else is here?" His voice had dropped, softer now, the kind of tone that made the hairs on my arms rise—not from fear, but something far more dangerous.

I tried to shake it off, scanning for another outlier among the polished elite, but my focus kept dragging back to him—to Nikolai, who had not looked away, who was definitely making his way toward us now.

"No, really," I muttered, pulse quickening, "I think he's—"

Fingers, feather-light, brushed along my jaw. A slow, deliberate touch. My breath hitched.

Jaehyun turned my face back to him, tilting my chin just enough to hold me there, his thumb barely grazing my skin. My thoughts scattered like startled birds.

By the Theion's, he was—

His black hair falling just so, his glasses adding something intellectual and devastating in equal measure, a quiet power in the way he watched me. Like he was studying, learning, deciding. Like he could read me down to the bone.

I wanted to—

"Jaehyun." A voice, low and edged.

The spell shattered. Jaehyun's touch withdrew just as Nikolai stepped beside us, his presence a weight all its own. I straightened, setting my glass down and forcing my expression into something neutral.

"I didn't realize Golden Coast was covering tonight's function."

His voice was smooth, the edges softened by years of practice, but the Russian still curled around the vowels, lingering in the spaces between words. His gaze slid past me entirely, landing on Jaehyun as if I were nothing more than a bar fixture. *Interesting.* That hadn't been the case when he was watching me from across the room like I was something to be studied.

This asshole was hot though. There was no point in denying it. Tall. The kind of height that made people take a step back without realizing it. The fine lines of a tattoo peeked just above his collar, black ink disappearing beneath the crisp white of his shirt. Broad shoulders. Sharp jaw. Dirty blond hair pushed back, except for the few stray strands that had fallen forward—annoyingly perfect, like they belonged there. A face built to be trusted, softened just enough to be disarming. A contradiction, designed to be dangerous. This was a form I would have taken.

"Would you have stayed away if you knew?" Jaehyun asked, taking a step forward, undeterred by the fact that Nikolai's frame now cast a shadow over his. "Afraid we might dig up some of those dirty little secrets of yours?"

Nikolai's smile was slow, a deliberate thing. "If anything, that would have made me come sooner."

Ah. For someone who prided himself on reading mortals, I hadn't seen this coming. The sudden shift in Jaehyun's demeanor and the way he gazed at me before—how did I miss how uncharacteristic it was? And now this little dance with Nikolai. Even though we were strangers, I should have known. But I didn't... He was using me, positioning me as a pawn in whatever silent game he and Nikolai were playing.

I bit my tongue, forcing words back down before they could claw their way out. Instead, I turned to the bar, lifting a hand. "Scotch, please."

Jaehyun didn't even glance my way. "Who's getting the special passes to the auction?"

Nikolai's eyes darkened with amusement. "Special passes? The auction?" His voice dipped slightly, like he was savoring the words. "I have no idea what you're talking about." He reached out, tattooed fingers brushing against Jaehyun's badge, lifting it just slightly. "But I'm sure whatever it is, this doesn't grant you access."

Silence settled between them, heavy with things unsaid. A conversation happening without words, a battle fought in glances and measured breaths.

I took a sip of my scotch, letting it burn down my throat. *Why does this always happen to me?* The thought came unbidden, dry with disdain.

Then, a man approached, tapping Nikolai's shoulder. He turned just enough to acknowledge him, then let his gaze linger on Jaehyun one last time.

"I'm sure I'll be seeing you again, Jaehyun."

Then his attention shifted to me. A long, assessing look. Not curiosity—calculation. The kind of gaze that weighed you like a coin in a merchant's hand, determining your worth before you even had the chance to speak. And then, just as easily as he had dismissed me before, he turned and walked away.

"How long have you two been fucking?" My voice was light, careless, as if the question had slipped out between sips of scotch.

Jaehyun didn't so much as blink. Instead, he reached into the chest pocket of his suit, fingers slipping out a sleek black card. A number was pressed into it, golden ink catching the low light. *Seven.*

"Long enough that he should know this wouldn't work," he murmured.

I tilted my head. "What, you don't like it when your boyfriend gives you gifts?"

"He isn't my boyfriend."

"Sure looked and felt like it."

A pause. Then a flicker of something—amusement, intrigue. "Are you jealous, Kasius?"

"Nah." I swirled the last of my drink before tossing it back, letting the warmth coat my throat. "Just annoyed that I fell for such a stupid ruse. You used me as arm candy to piss off your ex. Wounds an ego, while also building up one... I don't care to be taken advantage of." I set my glass down with a soft clink, then stepped closer. "At least, not without my permission."

Jaehyun didn't move. Didn't pull away when I cupped his face, fingers brushing over his jaw as I leaned in. My voice dropped to a whisper against his lips. "He's watching."

And then I kissed him.

His breath hitched—a hesitation, a heartbeat of stillness—but then his hand slid over mine, his lips parting against mine, soft and warm. I kept my eyes half-lidded, gaze flickering past him. There. Nikolai had gone rigid, conversation abandoned mid-sentence, his jaw set so tight I could see the muscle twitch.

A pulled thread. A slow unraveling.

This was reckless. Dangerous. I could hear Arestis in the back of my mind, reminding me of my mortality, of how easily humans burned when they played with fire. But by the Theion, it was thrilling.

I pulled back just enough to smirk. "How'd I do on the interview?"

Jaehyun's fingers traced a slow line down my wrist before slipping away. "There are still a few unanswered questions," he murmured, casting a glance toward Nikolai, whose glare could have split stone. "But so far... good."

He turned, tossing the black card onto the bar.

"You're not curious about what that pass could get you?" I asked.

"I saw two cards handed out tonight," Jaehyun said. "I couldn't tell which were which. That idiot just confirmed it for me. Now I have more names."

Then his fingers found mine, threading together as he led us away. The weight of Nikolai's stare pressed into my back, seething and unrelenting. The facade had done its job—ruffled the right feathers, stirred the right tensions—but at what cost?

A thread indeed had been pulled, and I had the distinct feeling I'd just stitched a target onto my own skin.

CHAPTER FOUR

"This isn't what I meant by agreeing to strangers with benefits," I murmured into the phone, slipping out of the lecture hall, the door clicking shut behind me. "You can't just summon me whenever you feel."

We had gone our separate ways that night. Jaehyun back to his life, and I to Kasius'. If it could even be called a life. A cycle of lectures half-listened to, of drinks that dulled but never thrilled, of meaningless touches in dimly lit rooms. None of that would have set my pulse racing personally. I had lived three thousand years, survived war and worship alike, and now I was tethered to this—a life that was numbing itself while waiting for death. So I did none of it—except for the one habit from Kas's routine that managed to entertain me, however thinly. College.

"Do you want to get paid? We never finished the interview," Jaehyun said. A car door slammed in the background, the low purr of an engine following.

I leaned against the cold stone wall, crossing my arms. It had been days, and still, nothing had happened. No threats. No warning. No shadowed figures waiting at the edges of my vision. Either Nikolai had been unaffected by our little performance, or I had underestimated him entirely.

"I'll take the silence as a yes," Jaehyun said. "Where are you? School?"

"Yeah. Actually in the middle of a lecture."

"Can you skip? It's not like you're on track for honors or flunking. You can afford to miss a little."

"Dick," I muttered. He wasn't wrong. I wasn't failing, but I wasn't remarkable either. I excelled in the things that interested me, ignored the rest. And today? Today didn't interest me.

"Alright," I sighed. "Where do you want me to meet you?"

"Main parking lot. Five minutes."

Then the line went dead.

The car door shut with a quiet thud, the weight of it settling like a punctuation mark between me and the outside world. I tossed my backpack into the backseat, stretching out my legs before glancing at Jaehyun.

"So," I drawled, "what kind of unorthodox interview are we doing today? And why couldn't this wait until the weekend?"

"An opportunity presented itself," he said simply, adjusting the rear view mirror.

That was when I saw it—a faint mark blooming just beneath the collar of the button up beneath his sweater, a shadow against his skin. My fingers moved before I thought better of it, tugging at the fabric, peeling it back like a secret. His hand shot up, gripping my wrist, firm but not unkind.

"Did an opportunity present itself," I mused, "or did you finally just get a break from your boyfriend? That explains why there were no repercussions from our stunt."

His jaw tightened. The hickey appeared to only be a day old.

"What really was the point of bringing me there?" My voice was lighter than I felt. "I thought I was being tested, that you wanted to see if I actually knew the people you were looking into before getting into the deeper questioning. But I'm starting to think it really was just to get your ex's attention."

The words tasted bitter. It wasn't jealousy, not really. We weren't anything. We barely knew each other. But I had let myself believe—for a moment—that I was more than a piece on the board, that I was truly of some use. As if I was doing something right by helping... And that stung.

I leaned back, exhaling through my nose, forcing my expression into something easy, something playful. "If that's what you wanted, you could've just said so. I don't mind being a pawn in your weird foreplay." I grinned, the shape of it masking the dull ache inside. "All you have to do is ask, Jae."

His gaze flickered, something shifting behind his eyes. "I had every intention of using you," he admitted. "But not for that. Well... not at first."

I sighed, resting my head against the seat, staring at the ceiling. "I get it."

"You're not mad?"

"Not really, I guess." The words left me with a weightless finality, as if saying them made them true. I had long since grown accustomed to mortals taking what they needed—Kasius had too. It was the way of things. We were used, then forgotten for something better. No point in dwelling on it. "I'd rather know I'm being used than be blindsided by it is all. Call it trust issues or something."

He studied me for a moment, then huffed a quiet laugh. "Here I thought I was going to have to make it up to you."

"Why?"

"You seemed like you might've liked the attention a little too much." His voice was light, teasing. "I actually felt bad after."

I smirked, tilting my head. "Clearly not bad enough to stop you from running back to Nikolai."

His fingers tugged at his collar, as if that could erase what was already written into his skin. "This was just a means of information. Nothing else."

Maybe part of me was jealous—not that I had any right to be. And maybe part of me was annoyed that I was being used. But if I had to choose, I'd rather be used than forgotten. Rather be a tool in someone's hand than a shadow left behind. I suppose, in the end, it didn't matter. I was both. Used and discarded. But that was my fault, wasn't it? For having expectations that never should have existed in the first place.

Why was I even letting myself get tangled in this? In him? The first human to catch my interest in this lifetime, and I was already unraveling. *Pathetic.* I should have known better—should have remembered that companionship was a fleeting thing, especially among mortals. Yet here I was, caught between wanting and resenting, between caring and cursing myself for it.

Fuck it.

I shifted in my seat, draping an arm over the steering wheel as I leaned in. "So, how would you like to use me today?" I asked, letting the words roll off my tongue with something dangerously close to an invitation.

Jaehyun hesitated. Just for a breath, a fraction of a second—long enough for me to catch it. A flicker of heat, the slightest flush on his cheeks, before he steeled himself, slipping back into the practiced coolness he wore like a second skin.

"Well," he said, exhaling as if he might laugh but didn't. "I did something."

A dull thud from the trunk. Muffled, struggling. A voice, barely contained.

I turned my head, slow, glancing at the back of the car.

"What," I said, voice calm, patient, and intrigued, "did you do?"

The empty car park stretched around us, silent but for the low hum of light fixtures. The trunk groaned as I lifted it open,

Jaehyun a step behind me. Inside, a man—leather jacket, black shirt, jeans—hog-tied, a strip of fabric gagging his mouth. Wide brown eyes locked onto mine, frantic, lips moving beneath the cloth in a language I couldn't hear. He thrashed against the bindings, the car rocking slightly with his struggle.

I exhaled, unimpressed. "So why exactly am I here?"

Jaehyun peered over my shoulder. "I need you to identify him." His voice was easy, unbothered. "He's been tailing me for days. Thought he might be one of Nikolai's, but the tattoo—" He nodded toward the man's arm. "Doesn't match anything I know."

I leaned in, yanking up the sleeve of his jacket. A raven, wings half-spread as if caught mid-flight, encircled by a ring of thorned vines. Not Ivanov. Not the Iron Bratva. I traced the ink with my thumb. Most gang insignias carried weight, layered with history, territorial pride. This felt different, less of a brand and more just art.

"Did you try asking?" I murmured, fingers curling under the gag. The moment I pulled it down, a wet glob of spit landed across my cheek.

Jaehyun sighed. "I was about to warn you he's a spitter."

I wiped my face against my sleeve, jaw tightening as I fisted the man's collar and yanked him up. "Alright, listen here, fucker." My voice dropped. "Who are you? Who do you work for?"

His lips curled back. "Fuck you." And then—another spit. My fist cracked against his cheek before I could stop myself, the sound dull and satisfying. He crumpled back, a fresh bruise blooming purple beneath his eye.

Dragging my sleeve over my face again, I turned to Jaehyun, still tasting iron-bright irritation on my tongue. "Why am I here and not your boyfriend?" I asked, voice taut. "I'm sure he could've handled this for you."

"One, he's not my boyfriend," Jaehyun muttered. "And two, I don't trust him for shit."

"But you trust me?"

He shrugged. "You haven't given me a reason not to." Then, a smirk, half-hidden. "Plus, you're a pretty big guy. Almost as scary as Nikolai."

I sighed, turning back just in time to see the bastard twist, muscles straining, ropes snapping free as he lunged up and stumbled from the trunk. He hit the pavement hard, rolled, then took off in a blind sprint.

"Shit," I hissed, muscles tensing to chase—

Jaehyun's fingers curled around my wrist. "Don't," he murmured.

I shot him a look.

"I put a tracker on him," he said. "Let him run."

I dragged a hand down my face, fingers pressing into the ache blooming at my temple. "Alright, enough. You're going to start answering questions, and I'm not waiting until your little interview is over to get them since we crossed into kidnapping territory." I slammed the trunk shut. My patience was thinning, stretched taut. I was too old for this. Too old and now too fragile for whatever tangled mess I'd let myself get dragged into.

I turned to him, arms crossed. "The night we met—those were Nikolai's men after you. They were going to attack you. Then at the Vassallo estate, same thing—his men, tailing you and causing us to crash. And yet you went back to him. And now you've got someone else following you. Are you just climbing into bed with dangerous men for the sake of an article? Or is there something bigger going on?" My voice was calm, but my irritation bled through. "Because I've been trying to make sense of this, and none of it adds up."

Jaehyun's arms folded over his chest, chin tilting just slightly. "Did you just subtly slut-shame me?"

I let out a sharp breath. "No, Jaehyun. I'm asking because you either keep lying to me or are keeping me in the dark. And from the looks of it, being around you can get me killed."

That shut him up. He looked away, shoulders tense, before turning back to face me. Something wavered in his expression—uncertainty, maybe regret.

"Nikolai and I used to date," he admitted. The words were clipped, matter-of-fact. "Back when I was still a rookie journalist. I'd just joined my father's company, didn't even know who Nikolai was besides the fact that he was some influencer or promoter or whatever. And he used me." His teeth caught his lower lip. "When he found out the CEO of Golden Coast Gazette had a gay son, he stepped in himself. Money and threats hadn't worked to get my father under Ivanov's thumb, so he figured he'd try another approach."

My stomach twisted. "And when you found out?"

"I broke up with him." The admission sat between us, heavy. He looked embarrassed, his hands balling into fists at his sides. "He clearly didn't take being broken up with well, neither did I to being lied to."

A slow, humorless laugh slipped from my throat. "So this is revenge." I shook my head. "You really did drag me into the middle of a lovers' quarrel."

His jaw tightened. "I'm doing this on my own. No one wants to touch them. Not even my father. He won't roll over, but he won't start a war, either. But someone has to. They can't just keep doing whatever the fuck they want and getting away with it."

I exhaled through my nose, watching him. "Would you still be pursuing this if he hadn't broken your heart?" My voice softened, but I didn't let up. "Because this isn't just about justice, is it? This is about being used. About making him pay for it."

His eyes flashed. "Of course I care about what they've done and getting justice for his victims," he snapped. "I had to lay in bed next to a criminal without knowing it. And now that I do, how the hell am I supposed to just let them keep spreading their filth? What if he manipulates another person like me?" His breath shuddered out. "I know I can take them down. I just don't know how to make an empire fall." His gaze flickered to me. "So when I found out you were related to the Vassallos, I thought—maybe you knew. Maybe you could help me get Ivanov to fall, like Legare did."

Ah. So that was it.

I stared at him, and in the back of my mind, I heard Arestis once more. *You really do have a savior complex,* he'd say. And a weakness for a pretty face in need of someone to use.

I sighed, scrubbing a hand over my jaw. "Get in the car, Jae."

He blinked. "What?"

"You said you put a tracker on that guy." I slid into the passenger's seat. "So let's go find him."

The sky hung low, heavy with the promise of rain. Jaehyun murmured something about the weather, his voice barely above a breath.

"The clouds are moving the other way," I said, glancing up before turning my gaze back to the dense sprawl of trees around us. "Might miss us entirely."

Weather. A conversation filler, the thing humans reached for when silence grew too thick. And I supposed, at this moment, it had.

There was no real plan, just the GPS leading us deeper into nowhere, tracking the man Jaehyun had marked. And then what? That part remained unanswered. Every time I asked, he'd say he'd think about it when we got there. As if winging it was a strategy. My instincts curled in protest. This could be a trap—an ambush waiting in the dark, a message from Nikolai sent through bruises and broken bones. Or worse.

Could I take him? My mind drifted. One on one, no weapons. I could take him. He wasn't that much bigger than me, and I am sure those muscles are just for show.

The car slowed, tires crunching over gravel as we turned down a narrow path. Ahead, a small house stood alone in the clearing. Isolated. Unwelcoming.

"Perfect place to hide out," I muttered.

"Or a perfect place to hide a body," Jaehyun said, voice flat.

I flicked a glance at him. "You planning on killing him?"

His hands tightened on the wheel. "What else am I supposed to do? If I let him go, they'll just send him after me again." The words came quieter near the end, as if saying them out loud made them heavier.

The house loomed, small and run-down, a relic of someone else's life left to decay. No garage. A shed slumped a few yards away. The porch light buzzed against the creeping dusk.

"No car," I noted. "But the lights are on."

"Maybe he took a taxi."

I exhaled sharply. "If that's the case, we could be expecting company soon. If you want information, we need to move fast."

We stepped out of the car, closing the doors slow enough that the sound barely disturbed the quiet. The only noise was the crunch of gravel beneath our feet, sharp against the hush of the woods.

We stood at the door, staring at each other, shoulders lifting in a shared shrug. Neither of us had a plan. Fantastic.

"Well, fuck it," I muttered.

I raised my foot, driving my heel against the door. The wood splintered, swinging open with a crack that echoed through the small house. Silence followed, thick and expectant.

I stepped in first, the space unfolding into a cramped living room and kitchen. Behind me, Jaehyun moved cautiously, his brows knitting together. Then, before either of us could react, the door slammed shut.

The man was behind it.

Jaehyun barely had time to turn before the gun came down hard against his head. A dull thud—not enough force to knock him out, but enough to stagger him.

The idiot didn't even have time to gloat. I lunged, tackling him to the ground. The gun fired—a sharp, deafening crack—but Jaehyun was already moving, his shoe coming down on the man's wrist, pinning it to the floor. Blood trailed from his forehead, but his grip was steady as he bent to pick up the weapon.

I pressed the guy down, arms pinned beneath my hands, body weight keeping him trapped against the warped wooden floor.

"You good?" I glanced up at Jaehyun.

"I'm fine," he snapped.

Good enough for me. I reared back and slammed my fist into the man's face. The crunch of cartilage breaking filled the room. My knuckles burned, but at least he stopped struggling.

"Who do you work for?" I ground out. "And I swear to the gods, if you spit at me, you'll need more than a nose job when I'm through with you."

Silence. But no spit, either. Progress.

"Got more rope in your car?"

Jaehyun wiped at the blood on his face. "Yeah. One sec." He disappeared out the door.

I exhaled sharply. "Arestis."

The air shifted, the temperature dipping as a sigh filled the room before its source did. Arestis stood before me, arms crossed, eyes scanning the place like I'd dragged him into a rotting sewer.

The man beneath me stiffened, his breath going shallow as his gaze darted to Arestis. Before he could even think about speaking, I clamped a hand over his mouth.

"Kasius," Arestis drawled, unimpressed. "You know we are not to intervene... What do you need?"

"Stay close for a bit. First—this place clear?"

He barely concealed his distaste as he surveyed the cabin, his gaze seeing beyond the shitty walls. "Besides Jaehyun, I sense no other humans in the vicinity."

"Good." I looked back down at the man beneath me.

"I need you to take that gun from Jaehyun, discreetly. Get rid of it. I don't want it traced back to him."

Arestis sighed. "I am a guide, not a criminal." A pause. "But I am a guide to a criminal, nonetheless." His wings flexed as he twirled a lock of hair around his finger, playful despite the hesitation lingering in his gaze. "So be it."

"One more thing."

He tilted his head slightly, waiting.

"Thank you, friend."

A faint smile, quick as a flicker of candlelight, before he vanished.

Footsteps creaked against the floorboards. Jaehyun reappeared, rope coiled in his hands.

"Did you get him to talk? Thought I heard voices."

"Nah." I slowly lifted my hand from the man's mouth.

"There was—there was an angel! I saw—"

I clamped my hand back down. "Damn. Must've hit your head harder than I thought. Maybe you saw the afterlife. Though, let's be honest, you're not the type to see an angel."

I forced him onto his stomach, binding his wrists and ankles with swift, practiced knots before hauling him upright onto a creaking wooden chair. He slumped forward, straining, but I didn't loosen the restraints.

"Who sent you?" Jaehyun's voice cut through the silence. The gun in his hand wavered, then steadied, aimed directly at the man's chest. "Why were you following me? What was the plan?"

The man only laughed, a short, breathy sound before his gaze flicked to me. "And he calls himself a journalist? Give me a second to answer before you start waving that thing around."

Jaehyun didn't give him a second. The gunshot rang out, sharp, final. The man howled, his foot jerking as blood beginning to seep.

"Fuck! Are you insane?"

"Oopsy, adrenaline," Jaehyun said simply, cocking the gun again, this time pressing the muzzle to his forehead.

"Alright, alright," I stepped in, fingers curling over Jaehyun's, prying the gun from his grip. He let go, reluctant but compliant. I turned back to our guest, lowering my voice as I pressed the barrel against his groin. "You want to keep talking, or should I give you something real to scream about?"

The color drained from his face. "Shit—fuck, alright!"

"Who sent you?"

"I was tracking his movements, his contacts. That's all." His breath came in quick, panicked bursts. "I wasn't supposed to kill him. Not yet."

Jaehyun stepped forward. "Then who gave the order?"

"Who do you think? Who benefits if you disappear?" The man let out a bitter laugh. "Not Nikolai—he likes his little fleshlight too much for that."

I pressed the gun down harder, directly on a testicle.

He gritted his teeth, hissing through the pain. "Dimitriy! Dimitriy Ivanov!"

I eased off, just slightly.

"He sees you as a liability. A distraction for his idiot son. The plan was to take someone close to you, hurt them bad enough to send a message." He scoffed. "But turns out you don't have anyone. No friends, no lovers—besides that psycho, and maybe this one too." His chin jerked toward me. "Your father's off-limits, so they figured they'd just take you. Wait for the right moment. Then—well, you can guess the rest."

Jaehyun didn't say anything. His jaw was tight, his hands curling into fists at his sides.

"Give me the gun, Kasius."

"No." I slid it behind my back, a familiar coldness brushed my fingers. The gun vanished, pulled into Khaos with Arestis. "He's still useful. But we can't stay here much longer."

Jaehyun exhaled sharply through his nose. "Fine," he said, voice low with frustration. "But I get the pleasure of knocking him out."

His eyes scanned the room, landing on a thick wooden cutting board on the counter. He picked it up, testing its weight, before bringing it down in a single, brutal arc.

The man slumped forward, unconscious.

"You're going to need to deep clean your car trunk after this," I muttered, lifting the dead weight of his body and slinging him over my shoulder.

CHAPTER FIVE

Jaehyun pulled open the trunk, and I dropped him in with a dull thud before slamming it shut. "We should have just killed him and left his body here." His voice quiet, almost contemplative, as if weighing the option like one might consider switching lanes in traffic. "It would have sent a message."

"Why do your instincts always go straight to murder?" I sighed.

"I'm just playing their game." He pulled open the car door, retrieving a battered first-aid kit from beneath the seat before walking over to the trunk. The kit clattered against the metal as he set it down.

I watched as he fumbled with the latches, impatient, hands shaking from adrenaline or anger or both. Gently, I brushed his fingers aside. "You haven't thought this through," I murmured, hands finding his waist as I lifted him up onto the edge of the car beside the kit. He barely resisted, breath steady but lips pressed into a thin line.

I tore open a packet of antiseptic wipes. He removed his glasses without a word, and I pushed back his hair, exposing the cut that ran along his temple. He winced as I pressed the cloth against it.

"The only way you get away with murder—whether it's this shit head or Dimitriy—is if you sink to their level. And if you do that, you won't be much better than them."

His gaze flicked to mine, dark and searching. He was listening, but he didn't want to.

"I won't stop you," I continued, voice quiet but firm. "I won't tell anyone, either. But if you want to do this another way, I can help you. You just have to trust me. And you have to start telling me the full truth."

Jaehyun exhaled slowly, staring past me, into the dark tree line. "I can't just sit here and wait to take the proper legal channels, Kas."

"I'm not saying that." I discarded the bloodied wipe and pulled out the wound closure strips, carefully pressing the torn skin together. "There are ways to get the same result without blood on your hands. But you have to start being honest with me."

His fingers curled against the metal of the trunk, jaw tight. Then, after a long moment—"Why do you still want to help me so badly?"

His voice was quiet, nearly lost beneath the rhythm of the rain beginning to fall. "All I've done is lie to you. Manipulate you. Put you in danger for my own agenda."

My hands rested on either side of his thighs, the cold metal of the car beneath them, grounding me. Rain beaded on his skin, catching in his dark lashes.

"You're too nice. And honestly, kind of stupid." He looked away, just for a breath, then met my gaze again. His voice was quiet when he spoke. "When was the last time you did something for yourself? Did what you wanted?" A wry exhale, almost a laugh. "I can tell you have a need to be wanted, to be needed—doesn't matter how you get it. But I don't need you. I don't need to be saved." He paused, swallowing. "You have a good heart, Kas. So I think we should end this here. I've been unfair with this exchange, and it's not even worth dragging a kid into it anymore. I'll pay you for your time and the rest of the trouble I've caused. The medical bill too. You probably spent money on that suit, I can, uh—"

"You have a good heart," I never thought I'd hear those words, I laughed to myself as his words unraveled, one after the other. I couldn't help but smile at the honesty of it.

"What?" he asked, brows furrowing.

"When was the last time I did something for me?" I murmured. "Good question." I leaned in, letting my lips brush against his. A breath, a moment, the world narrowing to this.

Human emotions were a tangled thing, full of contradictions and half-truths, twisting in on themselves like a serpent devouring its own tail. I missed the simplicity of being a Daimon—desire without doubt, hunger without hesitation. Back then, I wanted, so I took. I needed, so I had. No guilt, no second-guessing, no fragile hopes waiting to be shattered.

But now? Now I felt too much, and none of it made sense. Maybe it didn't matter that it didn't make sense, just that I kept chasing those feelings.

We have been numb for so long... But this—*him*—made us feel something, even if the reasoning was fucked up. I wanted to *feel*. I wanted to stay. Kasius had been drowning, going through the motions, and I had felt it, the weight of his mind when I woke in this body. He was the reason I awoke at all—because together, our shared pasts, our jagged edges, could give us something more.

"What are you doing?" Jaehyun's voice was barely above a whisper, his lips brushing mine as he spoke.

"Taking what I want," I said.

The first kiss was slow, deliberate, testing the weight of the moment. His fingers curled into the front of my shirt, pulling me closer, his lips pressing more firmly into mine. The rain gathered in his hair, on his jaw, cold where our skin met, but his mouth was warm, his tongue warmer when it parted my lips.

Then—a heavy thump from the trunk.

On instinct, we both broke apart just long enough to shout, "Fuck off."

Jaehyun shook his head, laughter spilling from his lips as he ran a hand through his soaked hair. "Should we take this somewhere else?" His gaze flicked toward the cabin, then back to me, considering. "Mm. Not there."

I lifted him with ease, opening the backseat door before settling him inside. He shifted backward, making room as I climbed in after him, shutting out the rain and the rest of the world with it.

Kneeling somewhere between the seat and the floor, I peeled off my soaked shirt, letting it drop beside me.

Jaehyun stared. His hands braced behind him, shoulders taut as he took me in. "Why do you look like that?" His voice was somewhere between accusation and awe, a flush creeping up his neck.

I smirked. "Sorry, does this ruin your habit of calling me 'kid' all the time?"

"Well, yeah, kinda makes it weird now that I *really* want to fuck you." His eyes flickered over me, sharp and searching. "If I knew you looked like that underneath..." His words trailed off, unfinished, as his fingers curled around the back of my neck, dragging me down into a kiss.

I sank into him, into the warmth of his mouth, his lips parting easily against mine. A slow hunger, the kind that built rather than consumed.

"Do you have a condom?" he murmured against my lips.

I paused. "Uh, no."

His head tilted back against the seat, eyes half-lidded. "I thought college kids—sorry, *adults*—always carried condoms." A pause. "Don't tell me you're a virgin."

A laugh bubbled up, unbidden. "I have fucked creatures you couldn't begin to imagine. This body, however, just hasn't had sex since I've occupied it."

He pulled back, blinking. "What?"

"Joking." I grinned, brushing it off. "But we can wait for another time." My voice softened, the edge of amusement fading into something else.

"Don't ruin the moment by trying to be sweet," he muttered. "Just fuck me."

He tugged off his sweater, and I helped with the rest. The sound of the rain filled the silence, steady against the roof, a rhythm in the quiet.

I drank him in, the last light of the setting sun gilding his skin in molten gold. I have seen many creations in my time. Yet, nothing I had ever witnessed compared to him. Every line seemed carved with impossible precision, as if some patient hand had traced him into existence with both devotion and desire. It was difficult not to see him as art made flesh, a masterpiece breathed into being by the Theion's will.

"Stop staring at me." His voice was quieter now, and for all his sharpness, there was a flicker of bashfulness as he turned his face away.

My fingers ghosted over his body. Faltering as it traced over the hickey left by Nikolai, a blemish on something too perfect to be marked by lesser hands.

"I want to erase all of him that lingers on you."

Jaehyun's lips curved, slow and knowing. "What, still jealous?"

"Jealous of what?" I murmured. "He's so fucken replaceable. And I intend to prove it."

I pressed my mouth to the mark, teeth grazing over it before taking the skin between my lips, sucking slow and deep until Nikolai's claim was nothing but a ghost beneath mine. My tongue traced along his throat, heat blooming where I kissed, another bruise rising beneath my mouth.

His back arched, breath stuttering as his cock pressed against my stomach, slick warmth smearing against my skin. A moan slipped from him as my lips closed around his nipple, tongue flicking over the sensitive bud. He writhed beneath me, hips lifting, body eager, desperate.

"Kas," he gasped, voice thin with need. "There was only one hickey. You can fuck me now."

I pressed him down, fingers digging into his hips, pinning him against the seat.

"The next time you're hard, I want you to think of me," I murmured, lips skimming down the taut plane of his stomach, tasting his skin. "My touch. My mouth. How much you want me." My tongue traced the dip of his hip, my teeth sinking in just enough to leave proof of my presence.

He shuddered beneath me, trying to lift his hips, to grind against me, but I held him still, smirking at his frustration. Was it cruel? Maybe. But was it so wrong to want to be the first thing someone thought of when they ached for pleasure? To carve myself into him so deeply he couldn't imagine another?

My cock throbbed, painfully hard in my jeans—I'd been straining since the moment our lips met in the rain.

"Kas," he whispered, the sound sugar-slick and wrecked. His fingers tangled in my hair, gripping tight.

I lifted my gaze, drinking in the sight of him—head tipped back, lips parted, chest heaving. Lust and desperation made beautiful.

"Say my name again," I said, voice low, my breath ghosting over his cock.

"Kas," he pleaded.

"Again."

"Kasius." His fingers tightened in my hair, urging me closer.

I smiled, slow and satisfied.

"Good boy."

I straightened, the crown of my head brushing the roof of the car as I undid my jeans, freeing myself with a slow pull of my zipper. The air was cool against my skin, a sharp contrast to the heat pooling low in my groin.

"Jae," I purred, wrapping a hand around the base of my cock. "We don't have enough time for me to get you ready properly. Think you can handle this, or should we wait?"

His gaze lifted from my cock to my face, dark and unwavering despite the flush creeping up his face. "I can handle it," he murmured, voice nearly swallowed by the rain drumming against the car.

He shifted onto all fours, lowering his head, fingers wrapping firm around the base of my cock. My breath hitched as his tongue flicked out, running along the underside, tracing my shaft from root to tip. My fingers found his hair, brushing it back, my pulse hammering beneath my skin.

Sloppy, eager—he took me into his mouth, his tongue pressing, swirling, slick heat engulfing me inch by inch. His glasses began to slide down the bridge of his nose, and the sight was too endearing for this moment. I slid them off, setting them aside on the rear deck.

My thumb traced the hollow of his cheek, feeling the stretch of his mouth around me, the way he took me in with that perfect, desperate want.

"Fuck," I exhaled, the word barely a breath.

It had been too long. Too fucking long. My balls were already tight, heavy with the threat of release. Not good. If I put it in him now, I'd lose whatever sexual appeal I had left, probably last two thrusts at best.

My hand slid under his chin, tilting his face up. My other grasped the base of my cock, only the tip still resting against his tongue. His eyes met mine, dark and expectant, swollen spit-slick lips parted, cheeks flushed.

Fuck. That's going to do it.

Shit. Shit. Don't cum. Don't—

Homework. Think about homework.

The overload principle states that in order to gain strength, muscles must be pushed beyond their normal workload—

Fuck. Not helping.

ATP resynthesis occurs primarily through the phosphagen system during short bursts of high-intensity exercise—

Still dangerously close.

Jaehyun sucked lightly at the tip, his tongue flicking just beneath the ridge, and my hips jerked forward on instinct. His fingers dug into my thigh. My vision blurred at the edges.

Fast-twitch muscle fibers generate more force but fatigue quicker than slow-twitch fibers—

Pull yourself together.

I pulled back, his lips slick and parted, a thread of heat still lingering where his mouth had been. My cock throbbed, aching, the sharp edge of release coiling tight at the base of my spine.

I slid my hand up the length of my shaft, fingers firm as they closed around the swollen head. A sharp squeeze—pressure cutting through pleasure like a blade. The impending rush stilled, held at bay by sheer force of will. The ache remained, pulsing, demanding, but the cresting wave of release faltered, retreating just enough to keep me teetering on the edge. My breath was ragged, my body taut with restraint, every nerve lit with the cruel pleasure of denial.

"Present yourself to me," I murmured. "Hands on the console."

He obeyed without hesitation, his breath ragged, his body taut with anticipation. I moved behind him, spreading my thighs wide as I pulled him back against me. His legs slotted over mine, his skin fever-warm where it met mine. One hand steadied my cock, the other guided him, positioning his hips so the slickened head of my dick pressed flush against the tight ring of muscle.

"Wait—I have lube." His voice came out sheepish, a guilty little admission as he leaned away from me. The sudden absence of his weight felt like a cruel tease, my body aching at the distance, wanting him back where he belonged.

I watched as he reached for the glove compartment, fingers fumbling before producing a small bottle of lube. My brows rose, a laugh already slipping from me. "You have lube in your car? Really?" My voice was light, playful.

He glanced back at me, face tinged pink, lips pressed thin in a way that only made him look more boyish. "Are you slut-shaming again?"

"No..." I drawled, the word laced with a grin. "Of course not. Just applauding your... readiness." I chuckled softly, taking the bottle from his hand. The cap clicked open and then came the shock of cold as the slick ran over my dick.

It took only a second to coat myself, but that was all the time he allowed. He was already shifting back into place, eagerness etched in every movement. His thighs trembled with anticipation as he hovered above me, his ass poised over my lap. Then the head of my cock pressed against his hole again.

"Is this how you've been wanting to use me?"

"Y-yes," he gasped, voice trembling. His hips twitched, then lowered—slow, deliberate—as he fought to take me in. A broken moan escaped him as he stretched around me, his body yielding, opening.

My fingers dug into the plush flesh of his ass, spreading him wider, watching as his body swallowed me inch by inch. Heat, pressure—he clenched around me like a vice, and I exhaled through gritted teeth, fighting the instinct to thrust.

"Keep going," I rasped, my voice rough with the strain of holding back. "Keep using me." He shuddered, adjusting, then moved again—another inch, then another. His descent was torturous, each motion a test of my control. He picked up pace, his body learning the rhythm, taking more, taking all.

My hand trailed up, slipping over Jae's throat, my fingers curling around the column of it as I pulled him back against me. He gasped, body pliant, but he still rocked against me, desperate, greedy.

"Look at yourself," I murmured. My gaze flicked to the rearview mirror, and his followed, our eyes meeting in the reflection. "Don't ever forget how you look when you take me. How it makes you feel."

His lips parted, breath shallow, pupils blown wide. I wrapped a hand around his cock, stroking him in time with the slow roll of my hips. The tension in his thighs, the way he clenched around me, told me he was close. So was I.

His fingers curled tight around the headrests, knuckles paling, his body shuddering as he took me deeper, held me there. My restraint wavered, then shattered, pleasure crashing over me in hot, overwhelming waves. I came inside him, hips jerking as I rode out the high, my grip still firm around his cock, pulling him along with me.

"Shit—" His voice broke as he came. His high didn't last long. Pleasure melted into realization as he took in the mess—cum streaked across the dash, dripping onto the console.

His expression shifted, satisfaction flickering into reluctant amusement, then mild exasperation.

He shifted, ready to pull away, but I held him in place, arms locking around his waist.

"Kas?" He shifted slightly, hands draped over my arms but making no move to pull away as I rested my face against his back. His skin was damp, his breath still uneven.

"Just give me a second," I murmured, voice softer than I intended.

Fuck. What was this? It wasn't regret—was it? No, that wasn't quite right. I should be satisfied. I fucked. I came. He's here with me, not somewhere else. He used me, not someone else. And yet, this feeling clawed at my ribs, something unspoken and unwelcome.

How could I possibly want more? I shouldn't.

I think... I think I like him.

Heat rushed to my face, shameful in its intensity.

"Kasius, are you okay?" His fingers traced along my forearm, absentminded but soothing.

"Yeah," I forced a playful lilt into my voice, grasping at something easy. "I just—uh—ran out of stamina. Sorry." I loosened my hold, letting him slip from my lap. He did.

But the warmth of him lingered. And that was a problem.

Jaehyun's phone buzzed, and he glanced down before cutting me a look. "Why are you texting me? I'm right next to you." He adjusted in his seat, the seatbelt clicking into place as he turned the key in the ignition.

"Because we have ears in the trunk."

The glow of the screen flickered against his face as he reread the message, the corner of his mouth twitching upward.

```
J: Why do you want to know his address?

K: What better way to chip away at Ivanov
than to start with the very foundation? If we leave
this  asshole  on  Nikolai's  steps,  he'll  question
where the fuck he came from.

J:  Then  he'll  realize  his  father  was
meddling in his personal affairs behind his back.
```

"Exactly," I murmured, smirking as his gaze lifted.

Jaehyun hummed, a glint of approval in his eyes. "Smart thinking. I guess I do need you." He turned the keys, and the engine rumbled to life.

We'll see how long that lasts. The thought came unbidden, a whisper from some dark, buried place. I shoved it aside. "Ha. Yeah."

The city lights stretched and blurred before fading behind us. The road widened, then narrowed again as Jaehyun took an exit, leading us into another kind of isolation—not the wild, untamed woods but something curated, intentional. The houses sat behind high, manicured hedges, acres apart, each one a fortress of wealth and secrecy. The driveway we pulled into was long, the car slowing before the imposing wrought-iron gates. The AEGIS logo gleamed under the dim light of the fixtures, stamped across the chests of the four armed men standing at attention, rifles slung in easy, practiced grips.

One approached Jaehyun's side, leaning down to eye level. Another stepped up to my window, and I got an up-close view of his junk and his gun, both hanging a little too prominently. Overcompensating much?

Jaehyun rolled down the window.

"Mr. Ivanov is not here," the guard stated, voice flat.

"I wasn't here to see him." Jaehyun's tone was just as even. "I have a package for him." With a press of a button, the trunk clicked open.

A silent exchange. A nod. The second man peeled away to check.

No questions. No hesitation.

They dragged the man out, his bindings and makeshift hood staying intact. The trunk slammed shut, and without another word, we pulled away.

Jaehyun exhaled, the sound bordering on a sigh. "Well, that's going to send more than just one message. We might've just put a target on your back." A pause. "This is the point where you should walk away. Because from here, there's no turning back."

I turned my head slightly, the faint interior glow casting just enough light to catch the edge of his profile. "Pretty sure I became a target the second I stepped in front of that punch for you. Which, mind you, was my choice." I held his gaze for a second longer. "Besides, like you said—you need me, right?"

"Right." His voice softened, something unreadable in his expression. "Though I do worry about you. You handle this all too well. Unshaken. Like it's second nature." A quiet laugh. "You really must be a Vassallo."

Something flickered across his face, a hesitation, before he added, "Thank you. For tonight. For having my back." His eyes met mine, and something in my chest tightened.

CHAPTER SIX

"I've been feeling... anxious. Sad. Afraid." I exhaled slowly, watching the words settle between us before continuing, "Though I suppose fear is just another shape of anxiety. At least, that's what the internet told me. I'm still new to all this. You're the expert, so you tell me."

Dr. Moreau shifted slightly, crossing one leg over the other as she turned back a page in her notebook. "Let's backtrack for a moment. You skimmed over those thoughts about your ex."

I tensed, my gaze flicking to the framed degrees on the wall. Psychology. Cognitive Behavioral Therapy. Trauma-Informed Care. All symbols of authority, of understanding—though none of them could possibly account for someone like me. "He wasn't really my ex," I corrected, the words coming out reflexively. "Anyway, as I was saying this new person actually thanked me. And it felt... different."

Her pen tapped idly against the page. "You keep avoiding the past Kasius. Why do you think that is?"

I hesitated. "I... I don't know. When I think about it too much, I get these feelings I don't like having. Not toward him." I leaned forward, resting my forearms on my thighs, pressing down as if I could keep something from rising to the surface.

"It's okay to feel angry," she said gently. "It's okay to feel hurt, even toward the people we love." She slipped off her glasses, setting them down beside her.

Love. I suppose I did love him—not in the way he loved Philetos, not with the same devotion, the same reverence. But love was apparently complicated, more complicated than any of the feelings I was already struggling to unravel.

And I hated to admit it, but she was right about something else.

I was upset with Zayd.

"I did so much for him," I said, exhaling sharply. "Sure, at first he didn't ask for it, but then it became expected. And I... let it. I never complained. Perhaps I didn't want to."

Her gaze softened, but her tone remained firm. "You're making excuses again. Your feelings are valid, Kasius. Acknowledging them doesn't make him a bad person, just as it doesn't make you wrong for having them."

I swallowed. "I don't want to feel this way toward him."

"You also can't keep holding onto it," she countered. "It's affecting how you approach this new relationship. You're afraid—afraid of being used, of being discarded if you don't prove yourself useful. And because of that fear, you push yourself further, take greater risks, all to make sure you matter."

Silence settled between us, broken only by the steady ticking of the clock.

She leaned forward slightly, her voice steady but warm. "You deserve to be wanted for who you are, not just what you can do for someone. And you deserve to be in a relationship where the effort is equal."

Before I could answer, a picture frame toppled from her desk, the glass catching the light as it hit the wood with a soft clatter. Both of us turned toward it.

"Oh, gotta go, Doc. Thanks for listening." I rose, flashing her a smile—easy, practiced.

Dr. Moreau frowned, brows knitting together. "You still have twenty minutes."

I was already at the door. "Then next session, we'll add the time to it." I slipped out before she could protest.

Arestis fell into step beside me. "Shame you couldn't stay. Therapy is good for humans," he said, amusement laced in his voice.

I shot him a look, but he was already moving ahead, stopping at a door just down the hall. "We've got about fifteen minutes. Dr. Richardson has this chunk of his schedule carved out for his little coffee pilgrimage downstairs." He twisted the knob and pushed the door open.

Inside, the room was a textbook definition of comfort—muted tones, soft lighting, a plush couch opposite an armchair worn just enough to look inviting. Bookshelves lined one wall, filled with medical texts and self-help books, their spines stiff from lack of use. A small, sand-filled zen garden sat untouched on the desk, the tiny rake resting exactly where the therapist had last placed it.

I moved quickly, rifling through the desk with careful precision, returning everything exactly as I found it. Who would have thought Dmitriy Ivanov went to therapy? He should really get his son in here. Jackass could use some introspection.

"I could've done this myself," Arestis remarked, arms crossed, his gaze trained on the door. "I also could've just sat in on one of his sessions."

"I know." My fingers trailed over the edges of the filing cabinet as I pulled it open. "But I'd rather see and hear for myself. It's easier to absorb the information. And if something's missed, I only have myself to blame."

He hummed in response, but I could feel something unsaid lingering between us. Before I could press, he spoke.

"Hey, Kas."

"Yeah?"

"I didn't mean to listen earlier, but I had to lurk for a bit." A pause. "Unlike Dr. Moreau, I'm a Daimon. I understand." His voice was softer now, more careful. "Give yourself—and Zayd—some grace. No one thought Kakodaimons could even feel what you did. When an Eudaimon did, we weren't surprised. But a Kakodaimon?" He shook his head. "Neither of you could've expected how it would end. I think if he knew you were capable of loving him, he would have never..."

"I know." The words were quieter than I intended. A sigh pulled from my chest, weary, resigned. "I think my anger is misplaced. At the time, I never felt used. I never expected anything. I didn't even realize what love was until the end, and even now, I don't know if it was purely romantic."

"Human emotions are complex. Best not to complicate them further by forcing them onto things that happened in the Daimon world."

My fingers stilled. "It's hard, though. Our emotions, our memories—they're bleeding into each other. I'm starting to have trouble separating us. I think he's hurting for me, and that's the problem." A bitter laugh left my throat.

Arestis studied me for a moment before speaking. "The best thing you can do is set boundaries and have open communication with Jaehyun. Make sure you don't end up feeling used and discarded. Kasius was once in love, you know. It was young love, but..." He trailed off. "I don't have to explain it to you."

Kasius was in love. Once. High school sweethearts—the prom queen to his king. Until she cheated on him. And not just with anyone, but with someone who was everything he wasn't. It shattered his self-image. And to make things worse, he found out around the same time our father died.

"You're right," I muttered, closing the cabinet. "What a great guide you are, helping me navigate my love life." I teased lightly.

Arestis grinned. "Ooh, love life? So, you're in love?"

"Wrong choice of words." I chuckled, shaking my head. "Still not used to all these emotions, alright?"

My fingers halted on Dmitriy's file. I slid it free, the pages heavy with the weight of confession, of vulnerability carved into ink. A therapist's journal—old-fashioned, meticulous and a gift for me.

Flipping through, I pulled out my phone, the camera's shutter a quiet murmur as I captured the words that mattered. The ones that mentioned Nikolai.

This wasn't the most criminal way to do things, but I wasn't aiming for grand heists or cinematic bloodshed. Prison and death were very real threats now, ones I had no intention of meeting. I had a future lined up—one that might even include Jaehyun. But for that to happen, we both needed to stay breathing. Charging in guns blazing wasn't an option, but waiting? That wasn't either.

Nikolai wouldn't kill Jaehyun. But the thought had crossed his father's mind. That was enough.

"He's approaching the elevator," Arestis murmured, fingers tapping against his arm in quiet anxiousness.

"Ah, shit." I slid the file back into place, pulling a tiny mic from my pocket. Dmitriy's next appointment was in two days—I planned to listen in. But my gaze flickered to the couch. No way in hell was I going to subject myself to the sound of his ass constantly shifting. And leaving it out in the open? Risky. The last thing I needed was some overzealous janitor sweeping my only lead into a dustpan.

"Give me that," Arestis whispered, plucking the mic from my fingers. He stretched onto his toes, pressing it against the top of a bookshelf. "Better audio when it's in the open, rather than close but muffled."

I raised my brows. "And how exactly do you know that?"

He smirked. "Some of my charges have... unique hobbies. Don't ask. Client confidentiality."

With one last glance around the room, ensuring every detail was as we found it, we stepped out. Arestis turned the lock back into place, restoring the space to its untouched state.

As we made our way down the hall, his voice lowered to a teasing lilt. "Where to now? Your boyfriend's?"

"Not my boyfriend," I corrected, but the small smile betrayed me. "But yes."

The elevator doors slid open. A man stepped out—older, a coffee cup in one hand, his jacket bearing a nameplate: Dr. Richardson. I brushed past him, stepping inside as he disappeared down the hall.

Outside, I moved toward my car, pulling out my phone and lifting it to my ear. A soft static, then clarity. Crisp, unobstructed audio. Arestis was right—I'd have to thank him later.

I reached for the door handle—only for it to slam shut.

A hand, broad and unyielding, pressed against the frame. "Kasius, right?" The voice was deep, rough, unmistakable.

Nikolai.

"I was in the neighborhood and couldn't help but notice you were here too," he said, voice smooth, practiced.

"You can just admit you were stalking me."

He took a step back, hands sinking into his pockets as he let out a low, humorless laugh. "Funny guy, aren't you? I see why Jaehyun's been hanging around you. What are you, a new intern or something?"

I leaned back against the car, arms crossing over my chest. "Why the sudden interest? Jealous?"

His grin sharpened, eerie in its lack of mirth. "Jealous? You really are funny." The way he said it made it clear he didn't think so. His voice carried the weight of something darker—condescension, disdain. "No, I'm just wondering why an ex-quarterback is playing journalist when he should be in school, busying himself with little projects. Need to make Mommy proud, right? Keep that GPA up. Speaking of, she should be at work right about now, shouldn't she? I bet the two of you don't get much time together."

My smile dropped. "So you have been stalking me." My voice had lost its edge of amusement, settling into something colder.

He shrugged, lips curling at the corners. "I like to do a little digging when strangers start getting too close to my friends."

"Friends?" I tilted my head, considering. "Didn't he dump your ass?" I let the smirk return, slow and deliberate.

His expression didn't falter. "Is that what he told you?" His voice was cool, measured. "Word of advice—stay away from Jae. Pretty thing, but conniving. Manipulative."

I pushed off the car, stepping closer. "Or," I mused, "maybe he was conniving and manipulative with *you* because he simply doesn't like you." I gestured at him vaguely. "I mean... look at you. Looming over strangers like a discount movie villain because your ego can't survive not being the center of attention."

I paused, thoughtful.

"And, fun fact," I added, glancing toward the building behind us, "we're literally outside a mental health clinic. If you're feeling this emotionally fragile, big guy, they've got professionals for that."

His gaze flickered downward, and for a moment, I thought I saw something else beneath the smugness, the control. But then he grinned, wider than before, something sharp and ugly lurking in the curve of his mouth.

"You know, I don't really think you're all that funny anymore." He exhaled, as if coming to a decision. "If anything, you talk too much, kid."

Then his fist met my mouth.

Pain exploded across my lips, the metallic tang of blood spreading over my tongue. I ran my tongue along the inside of my cheek, testing the damage, then rubbed my jaw.

Then I hit him back.

"Ohhh, I shouldn't have done that," I said, lifting up my hands. "Sorry. You just have a very hittable face. Instincts kicked in." I shrugged. "You can hit me again."

He didn't need to be told twice. His knuckles met my nose this time, sharp and precise. The pain was immediate, a dull throbbing radiating outward. I swung back, my own fist colliding with his nose.

"Shit, man, sorry," I muttered, cupping my nose as warmth dripped down toward my lip. "I know this isn't how these things are supposed to go."

Truthfully, I'd wanted to hit this bastard's handsome face since the moment I met him. And, if I was being honest—

It felt *so* fucken good.

"I can't tell if you're just stupid or bold," he muttered, spitting blood onto the pavement.

"A little of both." I wiped my nose with the back of my sleeve, smearing red across my skin. My lips curled into a smirk as I squared my stance, fists raised. "I can keep going, asshole."

He exhaled, slow and unimpressed. "I'm not playing these games with you, kid."

Kid. The word grated against me. He was older than this body by four years, maybe, but my mind stretched back millennia, layered in memories older than his bloodline. And yet, I could feel it—the muddling, the way Kasius and I blurred at the edges, the way his temper, his fire, bled into me. But I swallowed it down, let my fists lower as he turned away.

"Tell Jae I said hi." His hand lifted in a lazy, dismissive wave, his back already to me. He didn't even spare me a second glance as he walked away.

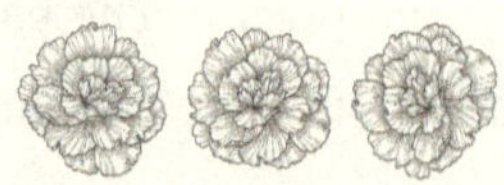

Jaehyun's eyes widened the moment he opened the door. "What happened to your face?" His hands lifted, instinctively reaching for me, but stopped just inches away, as if hesitant to touch something fragile.

"Turns out Nikolai and I have similar taste in errand spots." I forced a laugh, the sting in my lip making the attempt half-hearted.

His expression darkened. "Nikolai did this?" His voice dipped into something unreadable. His thoughts had already left the conversation, spiraling elsewhere. "I knew this would put a target on you." A quiet apology followed, barely above a whisper.

He took my hand and pulled me into the condo. The air smelled of coffee, still warm on the kitchen table, where an open laptop bathed scattered documents in a dim glow. The space was modern, clean yet lived-in, softened by personal touches. Old wooden bookshelves lined the walls, some filled with legal texts, others with fiction—worn spines hinting at late nights spent lost in other worlds. Plants filled every unoccupied space, vines stretching toward the light from the large windows. Framed photos were tucked among them—Jaehyun at different ages, with people I could only assume were his parents.

"I'll be right back," he murmured, leaving me by the sink.

When he returned, he carried a few cloths. He rolled up the sleeves of his slightly oversized sweater before turning on the tap, wetting one of them in silence. With a touch so gentle he pressed the damp cloth to my face, carefully cleaning around my nose and lips. I had thought I'd wiped most of the blood away, but apparently, I was wrong.

"This is going to bruise," he said, concentrating. "Your lower lip is swollen too." His glasses slid slightly down the bridge of his nose as he worked, and I found myself staring.

"What did you see in him?" I asked before I could stop myself.

He glanced up. "Hm?"

"Nikolai." I reached up, pushing his glasses back into place with my thumb. "What made you fall for him?"

He hesitated, as if the answer was difficult to shape into words. "He wasn't always an asshole."

I raised a brow. "I find that hard to believe."

Jaehyun chuckled, the sound quiet and wry. "Okay, he was always an asshole. But I didn't mind it, because he wasn't being one to me." He stepped back to rinse the cloth, then wet another. "We bonded over the fact that we both lost our mothers when we were young. Then over books, then film. He was good at making me feel seen." A pause. A breath. "But it was a lie. He didn't actually care about any of that. And his mother—she didn't die. She was paid off to leave, forced to disappear so his father could shape him into what he wanted. He's a liar."

I told myself not to be jealous. To communicate. I had been to therapy. Once. Technically, today. That counted.

"I'm jealous," I admitted. "I keep asking myself—if he was just using you, why is he going to such lengths now? But the truth is, I already know. They're the same reasons I'm here." I exhaled. "I get why he's obsessed with you."

Because I am, too.

Jaehyun was brilliant, sharp, and sweet in the strangest, most unexpected ways. He had an intensity that burned through him, and a mind that never stopped moving. He was a little unhinged, but that only added to the chaos and excitement I craved. And he was beautiful—undeniably, unfairly beautiful.

Fuck, I like him.

"I know I have no right to be jealous," I went on, words tumbling out. "I mean, we've only fucked once. Kissed a lot, but—"

Jaehyun started laughing.

Heat bloomed across my face. "Don't laugh at me," I groaned.

"Sorry," he said, still grinning. "You're just—so cute and honest." His voice softened. "That's why I like you."

The world tilted, slowed.

"You..." I swallowed. "You like me?"

"Yes," he murmured, the word barely more than breath as his lips pressed against my cheek. "Don't overthink it." A quiet pause. "I'm still in the middle of a bad breakup. I'm not looking for something serious."

"That's fine." My nose brushed against his, the space between us dissolving. "I'm alright with being a distraction in the meantime."

A hum, low and pleased. "Mm. You did say you only like being used when you consent to it." His voice dipped into something velvet-soft, his hands finding my hips, fingers curling into the fabric of my shirt as he pulled me closer.

I didn't need to define this, didn't need to place it in the neat little boxes people liked to use. He liked me. That was enough. I could wait.

I cradled his face in my palm, tracing the line of his cheekbone with my thumb before leaning in, brushing my lips against his. My lower lip ached where it was still split, but I didn't care. Not with him. Not now.

Jaehyun's hand slipped beneath my waistband, fingers trailing over my hardening length, his touch light enough to tease, to promise. He gave me a slow squeeze, and I exhaled against his mouth, my breath unsteady.

"I have a condom this time," he murmured, his lips curving into a smile against mine. No words were needed as he unbuttoned my pants, pushing them down just enough to free me.

"Me too," I pressed forward, forcing him back a step before my hands found his hips, lifting him onto the kitchen island. He let out a soft laugh, amused by my eagerness.

"Impatient, aren't we?" he teased as I reached for his waistband.

"Can you blame me?"

He lifted his hips, letting me slide his pants down, the fabric pooling onto the hardwood with a quiet thud. His skin was warm beneath my hands, his breath hitching ever so slightly as I traced the sharp lines of his hipbones.

No, I didn't need to define this. Whatever it was, it was already consuming me whole. I would chase it to the end of the world, to the edge of this fragile mortal life. I needed this—the heat of him, the way his breath tangled with mine, the way his touch carved me into something raw and wanting.

I had lived lifetimes, endured centuries, but in this moment, I was nothing but a body aching for him, for the way he unraveled me with the simplest of gestures. My hands found his thighs, my fingers pressing into warm skin, grounding myself in the reality of him.

I had no use for anything else. This—*this* was the only thing I craved.

I fished the condom from my back pocket, tearing it open with ease. The foil gave way with a soft rip, the sound lost beneath the heavy hush of our breathing. I rolled it over my dick, fingers tracing over the slick surface to lube them.

He had already moved himself to the edge of the countertop, legs parted, body open. My fingertip traced the tight ring of muscle, teasing, pressing just enough to feel the heat of him. His breath hitched against my lips as I kissed him, slow and languid, swallowing the sound.

"You're already soft for me," I murmured before pressing the tip inside. He trembled, a moan slipping free. "I suppose I'm not the only eager one."

His lashes fluttered, cheeks flushed. "Just put it in."

I pushed my finger in deeper, his body yielding, taking me easily.

"I meant your dick," he panted.

I let out a low chuckle, withdrawing my hand only to step closer, guiding myself to his entrance. The head of my cock pressed against him, teasing, before I gave a shallow thrust forward. Tightness wrapped around me instantly, pulling a groan from my lips. He pushed forward, his ass dangling off the counter as he forced himself to take more.

"Fuck, Jae," I ground out, fingers tightening around his hips.

I lifted him, the smooth flex of muscle under my hands as he locked his legs around me. His palms braced against the counter behind him, but I could feel his body surrendering, letting me bear his weight, letting me take. I pulled him down onto me, inch by inch, watching his lashes flutter shut, his lips part as his head tipped back in pleasure.

"You're so fucking hot, I can't stand it," I rasped, rolling my hips forward. He moved with me, meeting every thrust, body clenching tight around me.

"Fuck, come here."

I slid my hands up his body, gripping firm as I lifted him into my arms. His hands found my shoulders, fingers gripping tight as he wrapped himself around me. His breath hot against my ear, cock pressed against my stomach, leaking between us.

"Tell me how you want it—fast, slow, deep. Just say the word, and I'll give it to you." I murmured, voice low, rough.

His body tightened in my hold, legs gripping my waist as my fingers pressed into the plush curve of his ass, guiding him up, then down, spearing him onto my cock.

He moaned, voice wrecked. "Keep going—deeper. I want all of you."

His hips ground against me, not just taking, but seeking. His cock grinding against my stomach, his body shuddering in my arms. If he wanted more, I would give him everything.

Every lift of his body was answered with the pull of gravity, pressing him back down, taking me deeper, taking me fully and drawing me closer to the edge. His legs clenched tight around my waist, trembling, his fingers knotting in the fabric of my shirt, nails biting through to my skin.

"K-Kas," he moaned, breathless against my ear. "Just like that—don't stop."

His body clenched around me, sharp and sudden, and then I felt it—the warmth seeping through my shirt, the way his breath stuttered, the soft, broken sounds spilling from his lips. His cum filled the space between us, slick and hot. He turned his face to mine, kissing me with something raw, fevered, like he needed to pour every last ember of pleasure into me.

And then I came.

It tore through me, blinding, a pleasure so deep it left me shaking in its wake. My movements slowed, softened, as I rode the last waves of it, pressing into him, drawing out every lingering pulse. I exhaled, my body growing heavy, back bracing against the kitchen sink as I moved to lift him off of me.

But he pressed down, firm.

"Give me a second," he whispered, body completely slack against mine. I was still inside him, softening, and yet he stayed, holding me there.

My hands drifted over his back, tracing slow circles. "You okay?"

"Yeah." A quiet hum. "I just want to feel you a bit longer."

Heat curled at the base of my spine, rising to my cheeks. My arms tightened around him instinctively, and that was when I felt it—that quickened beat in my chest, insistent, undeniable. It had nothing to do with exertion.

He shifted, a lazy, sated smile tugging at his lips. "Next time, no condom. I like being able to *feel* you."

I chuckled softly.

Theions help me, this might be more than just a crush.

CHAPTER SEVEN

Fingers threaded through my hair, slow and absent, yet soothing all the same. A thoughtless gesture, but I leaned into it, craving the affection.

"So, you took these at his therapist's office?" Jaehyun's voice was quiet, half-distracted. He lay stretched against the couch, a pillow wedged between him and the armrest, one hand scrolling through my phone while the other idly played with my hair.

"Yeah." I shifted against the floor. "I was trying to see if he was careless enough to slip something about Nikolai—or at least any fractures in the family."

Before me, a file lay open on the coffee table, pages thick with names. Ivanov's payroll was vast, a network of loyalty built not on blood, but on money.

Jaehyun hummed, low and thoughtful, his fingers finally slipping from my hair. I barely resisted the urge to catch his wrist and pull them back.

"Dr. Richardson is paid so handsomely he wouldn't need another client if he didn't want one." He flicked to the next image, scanning the text. "Which works in our favor. Your hunch was right—he's comfortable enough to let his guard down. Not about the illegal things, of course, but..." His breath ghosted against my temple as he leaned over my shoulder, holding the phone between us. "There's a lot of tension between father and son. No surprise there. Dmitriy's only male heir is the product of an affair. Never quite good enough, never quite what he was supposed to be."

I exhaled sharply. "I almost feel bad for him."

Jaehyun scoffed. "Don't. We all have parent issues. Doesn't mean we grow up and start running crime syndicates." He flicked through another set of notes, eyes narrowing. "And it looks like our resident daddy-issues is the one who pushed for the trafficking operation." His finger traced a line of text beneath a clinical, careful paragraph.

Richardson couldn't write the truth outright—he was too well-paid for that—but the subtext was easy to read between the lines. A son hungry for more, desperate for wealth, control, power. An empire at his fingertips, but never quite enough. His father wary, hesitant. A push for something darker, something irreversible. Rumors already weaving through the underbelly of the city, whispers of bodies moved through his clubs like currency.

"If we expose this to the public," I said slowly, "Nikolai might assume it was his father's doing. Dmitriy opposed your relationship and attempted to do something about it. He's also opposed to this expansion. Would it be so surprising if he tried to sabotage him? We wouldn't even have to lay a hand on them. They'd tear themselves apart."

Jaehyun turned to me, gaze keen, a slow smile curling at the edges of his lips. "Smart and handsome." He kissed me before I could respond, and I felt the warmth crawl up my throat, spreading like fire beneath my skin.

I couldn't help him with Legare. That was its own ghost, its own long-buried ruin. Vassallo had pulled out a few years after Zayd and Silas were married, and its power had withered without its driving force. Silas had made sure it didn't collapse entirely at first, passing it to another branch of the family rather than dissolving it outright. But without Vassallo at its core, the name faded like dust in the wind.

"How are you so nonchalant about all of this?" Jaehyun's voice was edged with curiosity, his head tilting slightly as he studied me. "Researching your family is one thing, but you clearly weren't as uninvolved as you let on during your gap years. So tell me your secrets. Who are your sources? How'd you even get into that office?"

He leaned back against the couch, expectant, the soft glow of the lamp casting half his face in shadow.

I had rehearsed this moment before, shaped the words in my mind. I had always been prepared—for interrogations, for deflections, for truths laced with just enough falsehood to protect the truth. It had been necessary, as a Kakodaimon. Necessary for dealing with mortals.

But with Jaehyun, I faltered.

It wasn't just the fear that he'd think me insane if I told him everything—the Theion, Eryx, Kasius, the past that stretched like a shadow behind us. No, it was the fear of what would come after. If knowing me would place him in danger. If Arestis, my oldest and only friend, would suffer for my carelessness.

"You were right," I said finally, voice quieter than I intended. "When you guessed that I turned down my scholarship because of my father." I swallowed, shifting slightly, trying to steady myself before the words slipped free. "I shut down after he died. Locked myself in my room for months. I stopped caring about my friends, my future, everything that had once mattered to me. Even my relationship with my mom. With my girlfriend. He was the constant in my life, and then—he wasn't."

My voice cracked. I clenched my jaw against it, but Jaehyun was already moving. He slid off the couch, settling beside me on the floor, his fingers threading into mine.

"After a while, one of my friends dragged me out to a party. I got drunk, hooked up with someone, and for a brief moment, I felt something again. It wasn't real, just a distraction, but I chased it anyway. That became my normal. And I convinced myself it was enough." I exhaled, slow, measured. "Eventually, I went back to school, but the habits stayed, the guilt stayed. Guilt for wasting two years. Guilt for letting my athletic career slip away. Guilt that my mom had to work even harder to put me through college. I tried to help, picked up jobs where I could, but I just—" I hesitated, searching for the right words, but Jaehyun only nodded, understanding without me needing to say it.

"When my mother died," he murmured, resting his head against my shoulder, "I was ten when cancer took her. Too young to self-destruct the way you did, but old enough to grieve. To miss her. To know what was lost. I withdrew, pulled away from my father, and the wedge between us never really healed, even when we tried. Grief does that. It eats at you in ways you don't even realize. But at some point, you have to forgive yourself."

His fingers traced over mine, his warmth steady against me.

"I never met your mother, but I know she would want you to be happy. She would want you to take care of yourself. So don't hold onto that guilt," he whispered.

Something inside me splintered. Pressure built behind my eyes, my vision warping at the edges. When I blinked, the tears broke free, trailing hot down my cheeks.

Jaehyun reached up, brushing his thumb along my skin, wiping them away. He said nothing, but he didn't need to. His touch was enough.

I cupped his face, tilting him toward me, the warmth of his skin seeping into my palms. My lips found his, seeking, greedy. He met me just as eagerly, shifting forward until he straddled my lap. The coffee table groaned in protest as it scraped against the floor, glasses clattering with the jolt of my knee.

His breath hitched, sharp and wanting, as my lips grazed his throat. A sound so soft it sent a pulse of need straight to my dick.

"Hey there, big guy." His hands framed my face, his thumbs pressing gently into my cheeks as he guided my gaze back to his. He squeezed lightly, a teasing smile curling at the edges of his lips. "Just because you're cute doesn't mean you get to dodge the rest of my questions with your lips and dick."

He released me with a chuckle, and I huffed, letting my arms settle around him.

"Damn, you caught that?" I grinned.

"You're not in the mafia." His voice was quiet, thoughtful. "But something's off." His fingers traced slow circles against my shoulders. "I watched how you handled that guy Dmitriy sent after me. You never hesitated, never second-guessed yourself like a civilian would. You moved like it was nothing. Like it was just another day." His dark eyes held mine, unwavering. "Who are you, Kasius Nikolaou?"

I expected this. Of course I did. He was a journalist. It was his job to watch, to pry, to unravel the truth until it was bare and inescapable.

But this was a truth he couldn't have, so I offered him another.

"Is it cheesy if I say it was because I like you?" My fingers traced idle patterns against his back. "If I hesitated, if I left to call the cops, you'd have been stubborn enough to stay there. To keep yourself right in harm's way. So I figured—I might as well stay with you through the crazy and the danger. Because at least this way, I could try to keep you safe."

His expression softened. "So you're saying you helped me kidnap someone, threaten to shoot his dick off, and then squared off against my mafia boss ex... because you like me?"

I let out a laugh, shaking my head. "Well, it sounds pretty stupid when you put it like that."

The words barely left my mouth before he lifted my chin, his lips hovering just shy of mine. "It's not stupid," he murmured. His breath ghosted against my lips, and then he kissed me, slow and certain, like he was sealing a promise.

"You're very sweet, Kas," he whispered.

My pen tapped against the edge of my notebook, a steady rhythm against the silence of my thoughts. Across the room, the professor droned on, his voice a distant hum beneath the ticking of the clock above his head. As fascinating as it was to dissect how genetic predispositions could make or break an athlete's performance, my mind was elsewhere.

Dmitriy's appointment with Dr. Richardson was in ten minutes. And I intended to listen in.

One of the few perks of adulthood—I could just leave. No one could stop me.

I slid my notebook into my backpack, moving with the careful, practiced ease of someone who had slipped out of plenty of lectures before. No one batted an eye as I rose, weaving through the rows of desks, and stepped out into the hallway.

Earbuds in. Head down. I locked myself into a stall in the campus bathroom and sat on the edge of the seat, exhaling slowly as I turned up the volume.

"Good afternoon, Mr. Ivanov," came Dr. Richardson's voice, smooth and professional.

A toilet flushed two stalls away. I pressed the earbud deeper, straining to catch every word. My leg bounced, my fingers tapping against my knee as I focused. The feed was crisp—clear enough that I could picture Dmitriy lounging on the couch, the ever-present smirk of a man who saw himself as untouchable.

Most of the session was exactly what I expected. Dmitriy waxing poetic about his own brilliance, his own superiority. But then, finally—

"My son thinks he's some new-age entrepreneur," he sneered. "That he can do better than I did by cozying up to celebrities and influencers. A flashy little display, pretending to be innocent at its core. But these people have something to lose. The moment he becomes a liability, they'll turn on him. They'll bury him just to save face. You don't build an empire by playing house with the elite—you build it by lying in bed with men like me." A pause, then a slow exhale. "He's throwing one of his little parties tonight at one of those party houses. Boasting that it'll bring great things to our business, but really, he's just playing around while riding my coattails. Embarrassing. Having to explain to my associates that the party boy in the gossip columns is supposed to be the heir to *my* empire."

A party house.

Which likely meant one of Nikolai's clubs.

Dmitriy's voice bled back in, shifting seamlessly from business to nostalgia, though I doubted he understood the difference. He went on about his own father—the lessons, the punishments, the so-called discipline that had shaped him into the man he was today.

It sounded more like child abuse. But then, men like him always mistook cruelty for strength.

The sudden vibration in my palm nearly sent my phone clattering to the floor, the sharp chime of my ringtone jolting through my ears. I exhaled hard, pressing a hand to my chest. "Fuck, that scared me."

I glanced at the screen.

Mom.

Shit. I hadn't been avoiding her, not exactly, but I'd been preoccupied. Distracted. Jaehyun had a way of pulling me into his orbit, and time seemed to slip through my fingers like sand.

I swallowed and answered. "Hey, Mom."

"Kasius? Shouldn't you be in class?" Her voice was soft, warm.

I forced a laugh. "Well, if you thought that, why'd you call?"

"I figured I'd get your voicemail. But I'm glad I caught you."

Something about her tone put me on edge. "Is something wrong?"

"No, no, I mean… I don't think so. Unless—" She hesitated. "Is there something wrong?"

I frowned. "I don't think so?"

She exhaled, a quiet breath crackling through the speaker. "I went to pay the rest of your tuition for the semester. But when I checked, the balance was already cleared."

A pause.

"What do you mean?"

"There was no bill. It was paid in full."

My grip on the phone tightened.

"The name on the payment file was GCG…" A beat of silence, then, gently, "Honey, I don't mean to pry, but… are you involved in something? That was a lot of money. I just—" Her voice wavered. "I worry."

GCG. Golden Coast Gazette.

Jaehyun.

Why?

I wet my lips, already slipping into the lie before I could think too hard about it. "No, Mom. I mean—yeah, I'm fine. I picked up this internship with the Gazette. They work with the school, and they offer scholarships sometimes. It must've been part of that."

A pause. Then, relief. "Oh. Why didn't you tell me?"

I forced a chuckle. "You know me. My track record with jobs isn't great. I didn't want to say anything until I knew it would stick. I'm sorry."

"You don't have to apologize," she said quickly. "You're an adult. You're busy. I understand."

Silence settled between us.

"I hope you're well," she said at last. "I haven't seen you in a few days."

Guilt pressed against my ribs. "I'm fine. Just swamped with school. But I'll come home tomorrow. Maybe dinner and a movie? You still have Saturdays off, right?"

"Of course! There's a remake of that one movie you and your dad loved. The one with the sea creatures and the fish god." Her voice was lighter now, tinged with hope. Something in me ached.

"The Atlantean." I smiled. "That sounds perfect."

She sighed, soft. "I'll let you go. I love you."

"Love you too, Mom."

The call ended, and I exhaled, tension unspooling from my body—only to seize again at the sound of another toilet flushing.

Right. I was still in a goddamn bathroom stall.

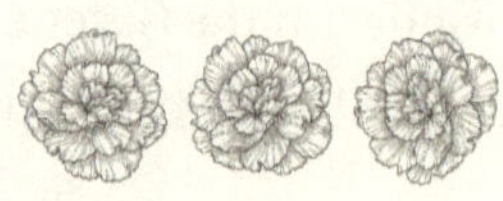

The Golden Coast Gazette rose against the skyline, all sleek glass and steel, reflecting the golden hues of the early afternoon sun. The building had a modern, effortless grandeur—clean lines, pristine windows stretching skyward.

I pulled into the parking lot, the scent of the ocean carried on the breeze as I stepped out. The entrance loomed ahead, flanked by towering glass panels that let the warm light flood in. Inside, the lobby was polished stone and quiet murmurs, the kind of sterile elegance that felt impersonal, yet undeniably expensive.

At the front desk, golden letters—GCG—gleamed from the wall behind the receptionist, catching both the sunlight streaming through the floor-to-ceiling windows and the calculated warmth of the overhead lighting.

Convincing her that, yes, I was here to see the son of the CEO took longer than I'd hoped. Skepticism flickered across her face, her gaze sweeping over me like I had wandered into the wrong world. But after a brief phone call—muffled words, a glance in my direction, a nod—I was given directions.

"Mr. Seok is expecting you. His assistant will escort you to his office."

The elevator ride was smooth, silent. The moment I stepped onto his floor, I could feel the shift. It was quieter here. Insulated. The kind of quiet that held power.

"Mr. Seok will see you in just a minute. He's finishing up a meeting," his assistant informed me, offering a well-practiced smile before slipping away, leaving me alone in his office.

I exhaled, glancing around.

It was nothing like his home.

The space was cold, restrained—dark wood, minimalist shelves, carefully arranged books that had likely never been touched. A sleek black desk sat at the room's center, pristine, not a paper out of place. Even the air smelled impersonal, the faintest trace of leather and polished steel. My fingers traced the smooth grain of the desk, then the cool metal of the nameplate.

Jaehyun Seok.

"Kas?"

Jaehyun had already closed the door behind him, his suit crisp, his hair neatly styled rather than its usual effortless fall. Contacts instead of glasses. A version of him I didn't see often—polished, poised, unreadable.

Still devastatingly handsome. Still him. But something about it felt off.

His eyes softened as he crossed the room, closing the space between us. "What are you doing here?"

Instead of answering, I wrapped an arm around him, pulling him in. His breath caught, but he didn't hesitate, meeting my kiss without a second thought. Warm. Steady. His hands settled against my waist.

When we parted, he huffed a soft laugh. "Please don't tell me you came all the way here just to kiss me."

I smiled, my thumb brushing against the fabric of his jacket. "No," I murmured. "I just... didn't realize how much I missed you until I saw you."

His gaze searched mine. "We saw each other this morning." His voice was gentle, careful. "Is something wrong? Were you not able to listen in on the appointment?"

"I did." I hesitated, my fingers curling slightly in his jacket. "It's just…" A pause. "Did you pay for my tuition?"

Jaehyun's expression barely shifted, but I caught it—the briefest flicker of something before his features smoothed.

"Yes," he admitted, his voice even. "I told you I'd pay you for the interview, didn't I?"

I narrowed my eyes. "That was way more than the cost of an interview, Jae."

He tilted his head, a playful smirk curving his lips. "Call it an advance. For future endeavors."

"Is that what you want to call it?" My fingers brushed the silk of his tie, toying with it, watching the way his breath hitched, just slightly. "Now I'm being paid for my distraction services?"

Jaehyun's gaze darkened, amusement flickering at the edges. "I think we both know you're more than a distraction." His voice was low, rich, pulling me in like an undertow.

I tilted my head. "Then what am I?" I leaned closer, our breaths mingling, the space between us narrowing to nothing.

He didn't answer right away. Instead, his eyes flickered over my face, lingering at my lips before meeting mine again. "Someone who's keeping me from work," he finally murmured. But his body betrayed him, reluctant as he pulled away.

I smirked. "Who says we can't work and play?"

I reached behind him, fingers brushing the lock. A soft click. Before he could protest, I had him against the wall, my body flush against his, lips teasing at the pulse of his throat.

"I have some information for you, Mr. Seok," I murmured against his skin.

A chuckle. "Don't call me that. Makes it sound like you're talking to my father."

I groaned, pulling back with a dramatic sigh. "Ahh, way to kill a boner."

He grinned, but before I could step away entirely, his fingers laced through mine, keeping me tethered and close.

I exhaled, lowering my voice as I recounted everything from Dmitriy's session. The shift in him was immediate. The playfulness faded into something sharper and profession. His expression tightened, his focus zeroing in, and fuck, he was so hot like this—serious, calculating, the weight of something vast behind those dark eyes.

I swallowed, pushing past the distraction of him. We didn't have much time. If Nikolai's event was happening tonight, we had to start planning.

Jaehyun turned, striding toward his desk. "Looks like we're going clubbing tonight," he said smoothly. "Do you need me to lend you the company card, or do you have something at home to wear?"

I huffed a laugh. "I'm starting to feel like a sugar baby."

His smirk was immediate. "Is it so wrong to be taken care of for once?" He shook his head, opening a drawer.

"Besides, call it reimbursement for a task I need you to complete before then."

He pulled out a folder, handing it to me. "Remember that event we went to for Senator Carrington? These are the names of the individuals who received a black card from Nikolai that night."

I flipped through the pages, skimming the faces, the names.

"Read up on them," Jaehyun continued, "memorize their faces. We need to be on the lookout for these people tonight."

CHAPTER EIGHT

"I can't believe you agreed to this." Arestis' voice barely carried over the bass thrumming through the club.

"I didn't just agree," I sighed, eyes drifting over the bodies moving in the dim light. "It was my idea."

Wealth could dress filth in finery, but it did not change the stench beneath. This place reeked of excess—of sweat and liquor, of desperation cloaked in expensive perfume. Even here, among the polished and the privileged, I saw the same truths. Hands exchanging powder in the shadows. Lovers pressing against each other with the fever of want, whether for pleasure or money. And those who lurked, watching, waiting, hunting for those vulnerable.

Arestis followed my gaze. "Aren't you afraid he'll spot you?"

"Nah. He'll be too busy."

Too busy with his hands and eyes on my man.

Jaehyun sat in a booth past the chaos, tucked away on a raised platform like a prince on a throne. And beside him—Nikolai. The asshole draped an arm around him, close, possessive. My lips curled, but I forced the scowl away. *Stop it. You're not dating. And this was your idea.* What better distraction than offering the devil exactly what he wanted?

Arestis nudged me. "At least pretend to fit in. You look too tense. You stand out."

He flagged down the bartender, cheeks pink with the thrill of playing mortal. "Two shots of... something," he said, holding up two fingers.

The bartender's brow arched.

"Tequila," I cut in. "Make it three."

Arestis leaned against the bar, swaying slightly to the music. His lips were curled in a pleased little smile.

"You look cute," I mused, tilting my head. "Very human."

"You think so?" He perked up, pushing a strand of hair behind his ear.

He was too beautiful, too finely sculpted to pass for an ordinary mortal. He could have walked straight from a movie screen, and no one would have questioned it. But I let him have this moment of seeming mundane.

The shots arrived. I took two, tossing them back in quick succession. The liquid burned down my throat, heat unfurling in my stomach.

Arestis took his, lips puckering in disgust. "That is foul."

I laughed. "Forgot the chaser."

"A what?"

"Two more, with an orange juice back."

The bartender set them down. I took my shot and chased it down with a sip of juice, savoring the sweetness that chased away the burn.

Arestis mimicked me, grimaced just the same. "It still tastes awful." He opened his mouth a few times, as if trying to rid himself of the flavor.

I smirked. "Didn't help?"

"Not at all."

His gaze flickered to the clock behind the bar. The hour was creeping close.

"We should move," he said. "The dance floor's near the stairs. If we're lucky, we'll see their faces without them seeing us."

I exhaled, shaking off the lingering warmth of the alcohol. Time to work.

His fingers lacing through mine as he guided me onto the dance floor. The music swelled around us, a living thing, pulsing through the heat of bodies pressed together, through the air thick with perfume and cologne.

I had Arestis study the faces with me, committing each one to memory. Four eyes were better than two, and tonight, I couldn't rely on Jaehyun without drawing suspicion.

"How do two men dance together?"

I huffed a quiet laugh, leaning in so he could hear me over the bass. "Your charges don't party?"

"No. Mine tend to be dreadfully boring." A playful smile tugged at his lips. "You've been the most lively one, Kas."

"That's tragic," I teased. "Gender doesn't matter—just do what feels right."

He nodded, determined, and began to move, his limbs stiff, awkward. It was almost endearing, but his beauty salvaged him. No one was looking at how he danced, only at him.

"Let's try this together." I let my hands settle at his waist, guiding him closer, my body finding the rhythm, leading him with easy, fluid movements.

Arestis followed, his hesitance fading as he matched my body.

"Look at you," I chuckled.

Instinct had my gaze seeking Jaehyun before I could stop myself. He was still in the booth, still beneath Nikolai's arm, but his eyes—dark, burning—were fixed on me.

I swallowed hard. *Shit.*

I had forgotten to tell him about Arestis. Not the Eudaimon part—that was a different conversation altogether—but the simple truth that he was here, that he was a friend, that he was helping us.

The anger in Jaehyun's stare was a sharp, electric thing. His stare seared through the dim haze of the club before he wrenched his gaze away, turning back to Nikolai with forced indifference. He leaned in, feigning interest in whatever conversation Nikolai was weaving, but the tension in his shoulders betrayed him.

I forced myself to step back, retreating from Arestis without letting the shift seem unnatural. My hands slid away from his waist, my fingers curling into my palms to quiet the nerves rising in my chest.

"So far, no one's gone upstairs to the private area," I murmured. "Keep your eyes on the floor."

Arestis nodded, his smile bright, unburdened. "Got it."

It was almost strange—watching an Eudaimon have fun again. This was how it used to be. When they were allowed to indulge in mortal pastimes, when they tangled themselves in the lives of mortals, not just as distant guides, but as part of them. Understanding them.

They had always been drawn to art in all its forms. And here, in the thrumming dark, in the haze of music and movement, Arestis looked like something from another time. Something forgotten, something free.

Arestis tapped my shoulder, his gaze shifting slightly to the side. I followed it carefully, keeping my movements slow, my attention casual. There—one of them. Blonde, mid-to-late twenties, gorgeous in the way that made her presence here unsurprising. But if anyone knew what she was really here for, they might be shocked. She wasn't interested in the drinks, the dancing, or the indulgent atmosphere. She was here for the business conducted upstairs—the kind that dealt in flesh.

I glanced toward Nikolai, but he didn't notice her arrival. He was too consumed, his mouth pressed against flesh he had no right to touch.

Focus.

"Another," Arestis whispered.

A man this time. Late forties, expensive suit, the posture of a politician who thought himself untouchable. I watched as he strode toward the stairs, flashing one of the small black cards to security before slipping past.

Then another. A younger man, same careful confidence.

"How disappointing humans are," I murmured, exhaling slowly as he followed the others.

Down on the main floor, a man approached Nikolai's booth—one of his security team, no doubt letting him know that his guests had arrived. Nikolai started to move, but Jaehyun caught his hand, the playful curve of his lips softening the moment. He leaned in, said something, and just like that, Nikolai let him take the lead. The meeting he'd been meant to have was temporarily on hold as Jaehyun pulled him toward the dance floor.

That's my opening.

I reached into my pocket, fingers brushing against the black card. It was a near-perfect duplicate of the one Nikolai had tried to give Jaehyun. If this didn't work, I had a backup—no, not just a backup, but an entirely different plan. One I couldn't tell Jae about because it involved Arestis.

Keeping my steps steady, I made my way toward the stairs. The bouncer took the card without hesitation, barely glancing at it before stepping aside. Too easy.

Still, I hesitated. Just for a moment. My gaze drifted through the crowd, searching for Arestis, but he had already disappeared. And then, against my better judgment, my eyes found Jaehyun.

He was still with Nikolai, their bodies close, moving in sync. Jaehyun's arms rested loosely over his shoulders, his head tilted in, his lips curling as if he was whispering something meant only for him. It didn't look forced.

A sharp, twisting feeling coiled in my chest. Anger. Sadness. Longing.

What if I was just a distraction? A convenient rebound before things settled? I wasn't like Nikolai. Not in appearance, not in status, not in personality. What if I wasn't Jaehyun's type at all?

I forced myself to look away. To focus on the reason we were here in the first place.

At the top of the stairs, a man motioned toward a room at the end of the hall. Instead, I slipped into a nearby bathroom. A moment later, Arestis was there, stepping out of Khaos to join me.

I handed him my phone. "You remember how to use it?" I pressed the button, showing him again. "Press this to turn it on, then the red button to record."

"I got it." He waved me off.

"You don't have to film the whole thing. Just get those three on camera—Nikolai, and the reason they're all here. Once you have enough, get out."

Arestis nodded once. Then, without another word, he was gone.

I waited. And waited. And waited. Time stretched unbearably thin, each second dragging like it was meant to test my patience. I shouldn't have been nervous. Arestis was immortal, a Eudaimon. Nothing could touch him if he didn't allow it. He could disappear before anyone laid a hand on him. And the footage? If we didn't get what we needed, I could adapt. We always adapted.

So why did my fingers flex against the sink like I was trying to ground myself? Was it nerves, or was it something else? If we pulled this off, we'd be one step closer to tearing down the Iron Bratva and AEGIS. And if we played this right, Ivanov would go down with them.

I exhaled, slow and steady.

If I were still a Kakodaimon, I wouldn't have to wait. I could make an accident happen. A gas leak, a fire, a snapped neck in the dark. Dmitriy and Nikolai gone in an instant, and no one would question it. A tragedy, an act of God as the mortals say.

"Got it," Arestis's voice was a hushed whisper, breaking through my thoughts.

I turned to him, taking the phone from his hand. "Is it trafficking?"

He only nodded, sorrow dimming the usual light in his eyes. Guilt settled in my chest. Eudaimons weren't meant to witness this—weren't meant to fully understand it. The Theion ensured balance, but that balance kept them shielded from the worst of humanity. And now, because of me, Arestis had seen it firsthand.

"How many?" I asked.

"Six. Adults, thankfully, but young. Eighteen, maybe twenty. All scared." His jaw feathered as he met my gaze, something dark simmering beneath his usual light. I knew that look. If I was myself, really myself, I could do something about it. But I wasn't. Not in this body.

I dragged a hand down my face, slipping the phone into my pocket. "Tell me about the room."

He shifted, refocusing. "There are two separate rooms off the main one. One exit leads back into the club—the one you were directed to. But one of the side rooms has an emergency exit. Leads to a fire escape."

"Where do they keep the victims?"

"The fire escape room."

"They keep them in that room? ...Probably so they can move them without anyone noticing." I tapped my fingers against my thigh. "How far's the fire escape?"

He gestured to the wall beside us. "Runs along this side."

"Can you get me a gun?"

Without hesitation, he pulled one out and handed it to me.

I blinked. "Is this the same one from that guy?"

"I didn't know what to do with it! I'm not a criminal!"

I sighed, tucking it into the back of my waistband. "Alright. I'll take the fire escape up. I need you to create a distraction, then meet me in that room. You'll escort them to the nearest gas station or diner. After that, they're on their own. Got it?"

I wasn't some millionaire vigilante living a double life, toppling the corrupt and saving the innocent. I was just a 3,000-year-old demon-like creature trapped in the body of a college kid—if we wanted to simplify it. And that meant there was only so much I could do without getting myself killed.

Relief softened his features. "Got it. Wait—how do I distract?"

I slid the bathroom window open, the cold night air slipping in. "You see that?" I pointed to the fire alarm. "Wait until I'm by the stairs. Then pull it."

He moved into position. "Kas," he called as I hiked one leg over the window frame.

I glanced back. "Yeah?"

"Be careful. You're—"

"Fragile. I know." I huffed a laugh before lowering myself out the window.

It was higher than I expected. But it was fine. Like rock climbing. Except without the safety harness. Or the safety.

I looked down at the ledge below. Too far for comfort. But there was no time for hesitation.

Fuck it.

I let go. My fingers caught the ledge below, but my grip slipped. The next second, my back hit something hard, and all the air rushed from my lungs.

"Fuck," I groaned, rolling off the dumpster lid and landing on my feet with a dull thud.

"Definitely fragile." I hissed, rubbing my ribs. "Savior complex, Eryx. Fucking savior complex."

This guy wasn't the brightest. In his defense, I could see why he wouldn't post guards here. It was an emergency exit—meant to stay clear, alarmed if opened from either side. Having men stationed would only draw suspicion.

But let's say there was already another alarm blaring inside. Suddenly, this exit became a liability.

My hand hovered over the door handle, my other gripping the gun. Waiting.

And there it was—the sharp wail of the fire alarm echoing from within. I shoved the door open and ducked behind the door across, taking a page from the asshole who'd clocked Jaehyun with this very gun.

The "special guests" wouldn't take this way out. They'd want something that kept them separate from the "merchandise." Nikolai would make sure of that. Which meant his lackeys would be the ones escorting the victims through here.

"Now what?" Arestis whispered beside me, pressed into the wall.

"Now we wait. Actually, you should go calm them down while I take care of the assholes. You're pretty and soft—it'll be easier for them to see you as less of a threat."

"I feel both complimented and insulted, but I'll take what I can get."

The door burst open, slamming forward. I caught it just in time, pressing myself flat against the wall. A man barked something in Russian. Unfortunately, this brain only had one language on file now.

Arestis stepped out, hands raised in a show of peace. The two men who entered didn't hesitate—guns out, aimed at him. One of them was still partially obscured by the door.

I didn't give him the chance to move.

I shoved the door forward, hard, slamming it into him before pulling the trigger. The gun kicked, the sound lost under the screaming alarm. He dropped, eyes open, body still.

The other man fired. The bullet grazed my shoulder, searing hot. I winced, lifted my gun, and shot him point-blank in the face.

A dull, wet thud. Then silence.

The victims—six of them, all young—huddled together, eyes wide with terror. Arestis was already speaking to them, voice low and reassuring. They weren't moving. Too afraid. Probably knew, deep down, that no one was coming for them. But Eudaimons had a way with humans, their souls naturally inclined to trust and follow.

I shut the door and turned to the emergency exit, throwing it open. Cold night air swept in.

"We're running out of time," I said. "Make sure they understand they're safe. But only for now."

"I did." Arestis started ushering them out, pausing only when he reached the threshold.

"Kas." His hand found my shoulder, and words that slipped from his lips—old, ancient, barely clinging to the edges of my memory. Warmth bloomed at my wound, flesh knitting back together. "Be careful."

"Thank you," I murmured, catching his wrist for just a second before letting go.

We moved. He led them away, disappearing into the dark. I circled back toward the front of the building.

I dragged the sleeve of my jacket over my face, wiping away the droplets of blood that clung to my skin. Then I shrugged it off, wrapping my gun inside before anyone could notice.

Outside, clubgoers flooded the streets, ushered away as fire trucks pulled up. The flashing lights painted everything in red and blue, sirens wailing over the bass still thudding faintly from inside. My gaze swept through the crowd, searching.

Fingers brushed against my skin, warmth sinking underneath the torn fabric where the bullet had grazed me.

"What happened?" Jaehyun's voice was low, edged with something between concern and frustration. His brows knitted together as he looked up at me, dark eyes scanning for more injuries.

"We have the footage." I entwined my fingers with his and started leading us away. "Sorry I'm late, I just got sidetracked."

His expression didn't soften, but he didn't press further. Instead, his steps grew more purposeful, guiding me instead.

"Where are we going?"

"Somewhere private."

A few blocks later, we ducked into a bar—smaller, dimly lit, less lively. The faint smell of cigarettes lingered in the air, mingling with alcohol and greasy food.

In the bathroom, Jaehyun checked the stalls before leaning against the stone wall, arms crossed. "Talk. What do you mean, sidetracked?"

I set my jacket on the counter and stepped closer, closing the distance between us. "There were six of them. Adults, but barely. They were blindfolded while on display, but if they go to the cops, it should be easy to identify them as the victims in the video."

"What are you talking about?"

"I set off the fire alarm." My voice stayed steady as I tried to get my thoughts together. "Nikolai was in fact selling bodies. I gave them a chance to escape, to get help. If we move fast with this video, this could work in our favor—"

There was a pout, a sadness in his expression as he listened to me, something I couldn't ignore anymore. It settled deep in his features, a quiet ache that made my chest tighten.

"Are you okay?" I asked.

He hesitated, then exhaled. "I know it's not my place. We know what this is. But I can't help feeling..." He trailed off.

"Feeling?"

His dark eyes locked onto mine, guarded yet vulnerable. "I don't think I like it when you smile like that at someone else."

A small, breathless laugh left me. "You're jealous?"

"Yes." No hesitation.

I pushed his hair back, pressing a kiss to his forehead, then another just because I could. "For a moment, I thought you stopped caring about me. It seemed so natural for you to be around him. I thought maybe you realized I wasn't good enough for you." My voice dipped lower. "That I wasn't Nikolai."

Jaehyun's deadpan was immediate. "The whole time, I wanted to stab him." He tilted his head. "And I don't give a shit that you're not like him. If anything, I don't like him because he's nothing like you. He's an ex for a reason. You are not."

I caught the shift in his tone, the weight behind it. "I'm not?" My fingers lifted his chin, his skin warm under my touch. "If I'm not an ex, what am I?" The soft flush dusting his face made his dark gray eyes even prettier.

"Mine."

My lips curved. "Yes, I'm your boyfriend."

"That's not what I said."

"Mm, pretty sure you did." I kissed him.

He exhaled sharply against my lips, then gripped my face, holding me there. "You're not off the hook yet."

Arestis. I sighed dramatically. "That was my best friend. I figured it was a better cover if I wasn't alone. I couldn't just keep staring at you and Nikolai all night, so he was helping me keep an eye out. I promise, there's nothing there. There's no way I could ever have something with someone else while you still exist."

Jaehyun raised a brow. "So if I die?"

I groaned. "Shut up. You know what I mean."

His smirk barely had time to form before I kissed him again, silencing whatever teasing remark was on his lips.

"You really are too cute. I can't stand it."

I grabbed my jacket, took his hand, and pulled him into one of the stalls.

His back met the stall wall with a soft thud as I turned the lock. My already ruined jacket landed over the toilet lid—an attempt, however feeble, at class.

"What are you doing?" he whispered as I undid the belt on his pants.

I knelt, my hands smoothing down the sides of his thighs. "Sucking my boyfriend's dick."

"In a bathroom stall?" His breath hitched, eyes wide.

I glanced up at him, fingers curling around his shaft. "Your body doesn't seem to mind."

He sucked in a sharp breath as I ran my tongue along the underside of his erect cock, slow and deliberate. His hand shot up, the back of it muffling the soft sound that escaped his lips, the other threading through my hair. His grip tightened as I took him into my mouth.

His head tipped back, lashes fluttering shut. The weight of him on my tongue, the salt of his precum, the way his thighs tensed as I swallowed him deeper—it sent weight to my cock.

Then, the bathroom door creaked open.

He tensed, fingers pulling me off his dick. I glanced up, bringing a finger to my lips.

Shh.

A shaky exhale. He hesitated. Then let me guide him back into my mouth.

The stall was too tight, the tile cold beneath my knees, the air thick with his unsteady breaths. I took him deeper, until my nose pressed to his skin. His hand slid to my jaw, his hips rolling forward, meeting my pace. A soft, muffled moan slipped past his lips.

The sink ran. A door clicked shut.

His restraint snapped. Hands tangled in my hair, guiding my mouth up and down his length. My throat strained, and I choked slightly, looking up to meet his gaze. Heavy-lidded, dark with want.

He was so fucken hot.

"Kas—" His voice broke, his body taut, shuddering. Then, with a low groan, warmth flooded my throat. I swallowed it all, licking the last traces from my lips.

Jaehyun's thumb brushed my chin, tilting my face up. "Open."

I huffed a laugh. "You think I'm above swallowing?" But I obeyed, sticking out my tongue.

A smirk ghosted his lips as he ran the tip of his cock over my tongue, smearing the last drops. "No. I've just jacked off to this image too many times. Thought I'd replace it with the real thing."

"So you have thought of me?" I rose, pressing into him, catching his mouth in a kiss deep enough to steal his breath. His tongue met mine, tasting himself on my lips.

His hand drifted down, tracing the hard outline of my cock. "Of course, no one else would suffice."

Fuck, he's perfect.

CHAPTER NINE

"Him," I said, tapping the laptop screen.

Jaehyun shifted in my lap, glancing back at me. "Him? Are you sure?"

The third "special guest" from Nikolai's auction last night. He looked young, and according to his file, he was—twenty-six, James Sanderson. Old money. A family of politicians, lawyers, and doctors. He was currently in law school, following in his father's footsteps.

"He comes from old money. That means high expectations to not fuck up. If we blackmail him, his family will do everything in their power to keep his name cleared, even if it means crossing Nikolai. This will put heat on the Iron Bratva, though not necessarily Ivanov. I could see Dmitriy letting his son take a hit, making him serve some prison time as a lesson. Or at least force him to take a step back from the limelight and focus on inheriting the throne. And in turn, this will cause it to crumble from the inside."

Jaehyun closed the laptop and turned around in my lap, setting it on the coffee table. "You're scarily good at this," he said, tilting his head, amusement flickering in his eyes. The sunlight filtering through the windows bathed him in a warm glow, making him look almost angelic.

I don't think I have ever seen a more beautiful smile, and certainly not one meant for me.

"Does that make me more attractive in your eyes?" I teased, pulling him closer.

"I'm not answering that and inflating your ego." He chuckled softly. "So how were you thinking of delivering the blackmail?"

"If I tell you, I'll have to kill you."

"You're dumb."

I smirked. "I have a plan. It won't trace back to us, and it'll be fast—which is what we need. One of my sources told me that one of the victims went to the police. She couldn't identify the place since she was blindfolded when she was taken to the club, and when she left, she didn't stick around long enough to remember the location. She's also from out of state, so that makes it even harder for her to pinpoint where it happened. But—"

"Please tell me there's some good news next," he sighed, resting his arms on my chest, his chin propped up as he gazed at me.

"Once her description is released or this goes to court, it'll be hard to argue that she wasn't the one blindfolded and on display in that video."

"That is good news." He exhaled, relief evident in his face.

"All I need to do is drop off the flash drive with a copy of the video and an anonymous note. After that, the rest is up to fate. I know you probably wanted guaranteed and immediate revenge, but—"

"No," he cut in. "I was blinded by emotions. This is what I needed. You were what I needed. So... thank you. For everything."

My heart stuttered. "...You're welcome."

"You're too cute when you make that face." He laughed, pressing a kiss to my cheek.

"Am I cute enough that if I asked you for a favor, you'd consider doing it?"

"Hmm... depends on what it is."

"Well, have you ever seen The Atlantean?" I swallowed nervously.

"You mean the mermaid movie?" He chuckled.

"Mergod," I corrected. "Would you maybe want to watch it with my mom and me after dinner with us tonight?"

"You want me to meet your mother?" He sat up slowly.

"Is it too soon? You can say no. I won't be upset, I promise."

"No, no, no—I want to." He nodded quickly, his eyes big and bright, the kind of look that made my chest ache.

I smiled softly. Theions, he was so damn pretty—definitely nothing like that little archive thief I met weeks ago. I didn't know why I had woken up, if it was fate, if it was the Theions' doing. But I felt like I was meant to be here. For Kasius. For Jaehyun. For me.

"There's one thing," I admitted, my lips thinning. "She thinks I'm doing an internship-like project for GCG. That it paid for my scholarship this semester."

Jaehyun tilted his head, considering something. "Now that you mention it... why don't you come work with me? You're good at this. And you have to admit—we make a great team. I promise you wouldn't have to do anything illegal. GCG is reputable." His voice softened. "That was rude and greedy of me to suggest, though. I don't want you to give up on your passions. I mean, you finally got up the courage to go back to school."

Silence settled between us for a moment. I traced slow, idle patterns over his thighs.

"Part of the reason I didn't go back to school right away was because of my dad," I murmured. "Not just because he passed, but... my dad was amazing. He showed up to all my games—fuck, even my practices. Football, sports, they were our thing. Don't get me wrong, I loved it too. I kind of had to pick this path. It just seemed like the only path since I felt like I was disappointing him in death. Going back for something related to sports just felt like the right thing to do." I hesitated, exhaling slowly. "But I think part of moving on is *actually moving on*—not clinging to the past. Besides," I grinned. "Your sports journalist? He's retirement age. I read his last article. Snooze fest. So I'm gunning for his job. Just being honest now."

Jaehyun laughed. "Mr. Williams is a nice guy. Just a little out of touch."

"Well, Mr. Williams better watch out." I grinned.

"So... we're really doing this?" He draped his arms over my shoulders as I slid my hands up his back, pulling him closer.

"Yeah, we are," I whispered before kissing him softly.

"Are you nervous?"

"Nah," I said nonchalantly as we walked up the sidewalk to my family home.

It looked the same—white siding, faded black trim over the windows and door, the same flowers planted along the perimeter—but something about it felt different.

When I first awoke here, there was a heaviness in the air, a sadness that clung to the space. It was why we barely spent time here. But as we climbed the stairs, that weight wasn't there anymore. Everything felt... lighter. Brighter.

"Are *you* nervous?" I asked when we stopped at the top of the steps, reaching to adjust the collar of his jacket.

"Of course not. Mothers love me."

"Do they?" I chuckled.

"I'm a very likable person." He narrowed his eyes in mock offense.

"Mm, I'd have to disagree."

His lips thinned, brows knitting together.

"You're a very lovable person," I corrected, leaning in to kiss his cheek.

His fingers threaded through the back of my hair, holding me in place as he tilted up and kissed me on the lips. I felt his smile curve against mine.

I pulled away slowly, fishing out my keys before unlocking the door.

The house smelled like herbs and spices, something warm and hearty. It had been years since she cooked like this. Normally, if we were home for dinner at the same time, we'd just order takeout—pizza, something quick and easy to split.

The place was cleaner than usual too. I guess telling her I had someone important to introduce did something. It felt like we were getting a slice of what normal used to be.

"Mom," I called.

There was a clatter from the kitchen before she poked her head through the hallway. She smiled softly as she wiped her hands on a dishcloth before resting it on her shoulder and making her way toward us.

"Hey," I started. "Uh... Mom, this is Jae. Jae, this is my mom, Lela."

"Jaehyun," he said, extending his hand for a handshake.

There was a brief pause after they pulled back, both glancing at me.

"He's my boyfriend," I admitted, scratching the side of my neck. It hit me then—I'd never actually told her I was bisexual. After our last breakup, we had experimented, sure, but nothing had ever gotten serious enough to warrant a conversation.

Something softened in her gaze, a glint in her eyes I hadn't seen in a long time.

"That explains why I haven't seen you much," she teased lightly.

A part of me realized I'd been keeping this from her—not just this, but this version of me, the one who was healing, moving forward. Maybe her worry for me had clouded everything else.

"It's nice to meet you, Jaehyun." She smiled. "Dinner's almost ready. Just needs a few more minutes in the oven." She turned back toward the hallway. "Kas, set the table. Show Jaehyun where he can hang up his jacket."

"Yes, ma'am."

The dishes clanked softly as we set the table, Jaehyun's hand grazing my back as he slipped past to place a plate of rolls in the center.

My pocket vibrated—once, twice, four times. I pulled out my phone.

Arestis.

```
A: (video)
A: Did it send?
A: I don't know what I am doing.
A: There's paparazzi too. Look online.
```

I leaned against the wall, crossing my arms as I clicked on the video.

"Oh... it's upside down." Arestis' voice filled the clip before the footage adjusted. The location was unclear, but those flashing red and blue lights were unmistakable. Camera flashes burst like fireworks as voices overlapped—

"Mr. Ivanov, Mr. Ivanov, do you have a statement regarding James Sanderson's claims?"

"Mr. Ivanov—!"

Arestis maneuvered for a better angle, capturing Nikolai being escorted into the back of a police car. He wasn't cuffed, but this was still a statement—the untouchable had been touched.

Jaehyun stepped beside me, eyes fixed on the screen. "It really worked," he murmured.

"Did you doubt us?" I raised a brow.

"Of course not." He chuckled.

I typed *James Sanderson Nikolai Ivanov Scandal* into the search bar, and sure enough, James had absolutely no crisis training. It was almost comical.

"He posted a statement to social media?" Jaehyun took my phone, jaw slack with disbelief. "What an idiot. There's no way his PR team can clean this up. And no way Ivanov will be able to shut them up now. What is with your generation and those damn crying on the kitchen floor apology videos?" His laughter was uncontrollable.

Even though I shouldn't have felt anything for him, pity edged its way in again. If it hadn't been for me—if I weren't tangled in the world of Daimons, if Arestis hadn't intervened—Nikolai would have slipped free, clean and unscathed. For all his recklessness, he was clever. New to the big leagues, yes, still rough in his independence, but there was an audacity to the way he played the system. The way he sharpened politics into a weapon. If he had been my charge, I might even have been impressed.

But this wasn't finished. Damage control would come, as it always did, and within hours he would likely be back on the streets, draped in the armor of money and a lawyer worth a hefty ransom. Still, that didn't mean we were going to let it be buried. Our work wasn't done. We had a wedge to drive further between father and son, and I knew better than anyone how quickly resentment in blood could topple an empire.

A notification dinged—not mine.

Jae pulled out his phone, eyes scanning the screen before his expression relaxed into something mischievous. "It's GCG. They need someone to cover this ASAP. Find any witnesses from the club that night. Are you up for starting your new job tomorrow?"

"There's nothing I'd like better." I wrapped my arms around him. "Boss."

"Don't call me that. That sounds like an HR violation." He chuckled.

I kissed his neck. "Okay, Mr. Seok."

"Gross. No." He laughed, lightly shoving my chest.

The weight of everything settled—not just this win, but the shift in my life, in our lives. The darkness was still there, but it no longer consumed me.

For the first time in a long time, I felt like I was exactly where I was meant to be.

NOTE FROM THE AUTHOR

Thank you so much for taking the time to read my story! I'd be truly grateful if you could take a moment to leave an honest review and rating on Goodreads, Amazon, or any other platform you prefer. Your feedback makes a world of difference for small authors like me. If you'd like to learn more about me, explore my other works, or check out upcoming projects, please visit https://elijahher.com.

Thank you again for your support!

OTHER WORKS BY ELIJAH HER

"Binds of the Forsaken"

"Her Majesty's Captain"

"Ascendance of the Forgotten Prince"

and a few web-novels that are only available on Tapas.

CHARACTERS OF RotF

Kasius Nikolaou (He/Him)
Age: 23 (actually 3000+)
Species: ~~Kakodaimon~~ Human
Personality Type & Sign: INFJ, Pisces
Physical Descriptions: Hazel Eyes, Dark Brown Hair, Shoulder Tattoo, 6'3" Muscular Build
Favorites: Dark Chocolate, People-Watching (with a side of judging), The sound of rain on stone, Apparently College

Jaehyun Seok (He/Him)
Age: 32
Species: Human
Personality Type & Sign: ENTP, Virgo
Physical Descriptions: Dark Gray Eyes, Black Hair, 5'9" Athletic Build
Favorites: Ramen, Iced Coffee, The smell of coffee beans, Photography, Sunflowers

THE DAIMON WORLD OF RotF

The world of *Renascence of the Forsaken* was inspired by Hellenic mythos surrounding Daemons and the multifaceted aspects of the Theoi, the gods.

In RotF, the Theion are the divine beings of creation, the gods. They are multifaceted, multi-gendered, and encompass all aspects of the universe and existence itself. Daimons are divine beings that influence mortals under the orders of the Theion. Their job is to maintain balance, chaos, and order. Eudaimons are meant to inspire, while Kakodaimons are meant to tempt. Neither is strictly good or bad, despite their own personal beliefs.

The divine realm is divided into three planes of mists. Aither is the realm of the Eudaimons and the Theion. Erebos is the realm of the Kakodaimons and the deceased. Khaos is the in-between; the dead pass through to get to Erebos, and the Daimons linger to watch over the mortal realm. In Khaos, the mists swirl through the land of the living unseen, unheard, undetected.

Mortal souls follow a cycle of rebirth, living new lives after death. The number of renewals is determined by the Theion, but all souls are finite. When their cycle ends, they are drawn to Erebos, where they rest in eternal limbo, endlessly reliving either their most cherished or most regretted moments.

A Daimon Short-Story

BINDS OF ARDOR

ELIJAH HER

ARESTIS

He moved like someone who had learned to hide his exhaustion behind a smile. The kind of smile that soothed fussy customers and softened endless shifts, but never quite touched his eyes. I watched him work, hands deft with the grinder, the steam wand, the steady pour. He wore his sadness like a second apron—tied neat and out of sight, but always there if you looked closely enough.

I shouldn't have been looking so closely. But I always did.

Rin Vang. Tall, handsome. The kind of brown eyes that made you feel safe, at peace. He seemed perfect. So perfect, in fact, that I led my charge toward him. They were both artists, after all. She found hers in the stroke of a brush; he found his in ground coffee beans and flour dusted with sugar.

But mortals are never so simple. Affection, attachment—they do not obey symmetry. No matter how neatly it should have aligned, it didn't.

Rin was glowing that day, though. Radiant when they finally met in person. A coffee date, naturally. They laughed that he never left this place. And after watching him for so long, I knew how true that was.

Could anyone blame him? Nothing made him beam more than his machines, his little art of pastries, his symphony of highly caffeinated drinks. But when the moment faded, I saw the shadow return. That loneliness that clung just beneath his smile.

I suppose it was that very loneliness in his eyes that kept me here, long after my charge's chapter had closed and moved on.

Today was like any other day. With my charges settled and quiet for once, I indulged in my favorite pastime—watching him from Khaos.

I perched on the counter with my legs crossed, palms pressed lightly against the surface behind me. From this realm, everything blurred and dimmed—the sounds, the colors, even the comforting scent of roasted beans. All of it muted, as though I were looking through water. And yet he was vivid to me. Always vivid. I watched as he moved through the last rush of the afternoon, steady even in his weariness.

But today wasn't like any other day. Beneath the weariness there was something else—something giddy, something joyful, so contagious that even I found myself smiling. I leaned forward, chin resting in my palms, unable to tear my eyes away from him.

After his shift, Rin would be going on another date. The messages had lit up his phone all afternoon, little bursts of anticipation he carried in his pocket. From what I'd read over his shoulder—yes, shamelessly—the guy seemed sweet enough.

Rin carried a single cup in his hand, weaving between tables with his usual stride. But I saw it—the lid wasn't secure, the liquid trembling with each step, and just ahead, a slick patch of floor waited like a trap. My chest tightened. *Oh, Theions, I thought. He's going to ruin his outfit before his date.*

For a heartbeat, the world froze. His stride, his easy smile, the dark coffee trembling at the rim—all suspended in stillness.

Before I could stop myself, I stepped forward. Out of Khaos.

The mortal world rushed in to meet me—the sharp hiss of the espresso machine, the hum of voices, the scent of roasted beans and sugar, rich and dizzying. And Rin—so close now—completely unaware of how close disaster lingered.

I reached for him, meaning only to steady, only to save. But the moment my fingers brushed his arm, my own balance faltered. My foot slid, the cup tipped—

And then his arm was around me.

Rin steadied me with surprising strength, holding me firmly just as the coffee splashed across us both. The heat seared through fabric, but I hardly noticed. Because when his eyes found mine—deep, warm brown, filled with startled concern—the world stopped again, and not for danger this time.

They consumed me, pulled me under like sunlight through dark water. And I thought, absurdly, that no divine creation I had ever witnessed could compare.

"Are you alright?" he asked, his voice softer than I have ever been able to hear through the mists of Khaos. Sweet. Addictive.

His fingers lingered at my side while my hand rested against his chest. Even through his apron and sweater I felt the firmness beneath. *Well.* At least I knew where those carbs went.

"Hi," I said, a smile tugging at my mouth before I could stop it.

"Hi?" he echoed, head tilted, his grin crooked in a way that showed the edge of a canine.

He was so handsome I almost reached out—

But before I could, he stepped away, leaving my hand suspended in the air, foolishly reaching for what was no longer there. Only for him to return a heartbeat later with a half-stack of napkins, flustered but determined. He pressed a few gently against my chest, blotting at the dark stains, while offering the rest into my hand.

"I really am so sorry," he murmured, eyes darting anywhere but mine. "I should've been watching where I was going."

That shy smile of his, paired with the faint panic flickering beneath, nearly undid me.

"I should remake this drink," he said, voice laced with apology, eyes flicking to mine like he couldn't bear to let me think less of him. "Please don't leave—let me make it up to you for the mess."

Of course, I could have undone the spill with a thought. Erased the stain, dried the fabric, made it seem as though nothing had ever happened. But I liked his attention—the way it lingered, the way it softened when it turned toward me.

I sat with the napkins still clutched in my hand, watching as he tugged off his apron, the damp fabric clinging stubbornly to him. Beneath, his clothes were nearly untouched. He moved briskly, light returning to his face as he crafted the new drink with practiced ease, his smile carrying him through. He handed it to the waiting customer before crossing to the door and flipping the sign to *Closed*.

Closing time. Which meant his date was near. But Rin was too kind to turn me away, even now.

"Please, let me make it up to you," he tried again, rubbing at the back of his neck with that sheepish charm that unraveled me. "Ahh, what did you order earlier? I don't remember—but I can make you that, or something else. Anything."

"You don't have to," I murmured. "I wouldn't want to keep you. I'm sure you've somewhere else to be—"

My words drifted away as my eyes caught on the machine behind him. Steam coiled wrong, pressure humming too loud. I stepped instinctively closer, hand lifting before I could stop myself, pointing just over his broad shoulder. "Is that supposed to be doing that?"

Rin stood before the machine, lifting the hem of his sweater and shirt together to shield his hand as he reached for the metal. The movement bared the front of his stomach, skin tan and smooth, a dark trail of hair dipping beneath his waistband. My breath caught before I could scold myself for noticing.

"You're going to burn yourself," I said before I could stop myself, stepping closer.

He laughed under his breath, nervous but stubborn. "I've dealt with worse. Besides, it's just a little steam—"

I was beside him in a blink, fingers brushing his wrist as I gently pushed his hand away. "Not steam. Scalding metal. Let me."

The truth was, it couldn't hurt me. I pressed my palm against the side of the machine, twisting the knob without hesitation. For a second, I thought I had handled it perfectly. And then—

The machine shrieked, hissed, and burst.

Foam erupted in a glorious arc, white froth splattering across the counter, the floor—us. Rin blinked at me through a veil of foam, his lips parted in shock before they curved upward into the crooked grin I had already memorized.

I stood frozen, dripping, utterly betrayed by mortal appliances.

He burst out laughing, shoulders shaking as he tried and failed to wipe the foam from his sweater. "You—" He wheezed between laughs. "You made it worse!"

And yet, even covered in froth and humiliation, I couldn't bring myself to care. His laughter was the sweetest thing I had ever heard.

"I'm so sorry," I managed between laughter, reaching up with the clean edge of my sleeve to brush the foam from his cheek.

"Really, I should be the one apologizing," he chuckled, the sound warm, easy. "Messes happen. Don't worry about it."

But then his laughter slowed, his gaze lingering on mine. His thumb lifted, swiping gently along my cheek as though he couldn't help himself. The touch was feather-light, and yet I felt it everywhere.

Our eyes locked, and in the silence that followed, I watched a flush bloom across his skin. A redness that climbed his cheekbones, soft and unguarded, more beautiful than anything I had ever been forbidden to touch.

"I'm Rin," he said softly.

"Arestis," I breathed, our hands slipping apart at last. A flutter rose in my chest, wild and unfamiliar. Scary, yes—but also thrilling, like the first beat of wings before flight.

"Arestis..." He tasted the name, smiling faintly. "I like that." His gaze dipped to the floor, only to snap back as he realized the disaster spread around us.

With a quiet sigh, he pulled his phone from his back pocket and typed quickly, the gentle *whoosh* of a sent message breaking the silence. When he slipped it away again, his smile was crooked with a nervous sort of resolve.

"So here's the thing," he said, scratching lightly at the back of his neck. "I really want to make this up to you, but I can't leave this place looking like *this*. And I definitely can't leave looking like *this*." His eyes flicked down at his foam-spattered clothes before finding mine again. "But... can I take you out tonight? If you're free. I promise—no coffee involved."

He cancelled his date. He cancelled his date—for *me*.

"I'm sorry, was that—did I come on too strong? I-I didn't mean to." His words stumbled, mistaking my silence for something it wasn't.

"No, no," I said quickly, clasping my hands against my chest like a prayer. "I'd love that. Yes."

"Really?" The warmth in him deepened, rising to his cheeks, climbing to his ears until even his fluster glowed.

"Yes," I whispered, my smile soft and certain. "I'd like nothing more, Rin."

And in that moment, I forgot the rules, the boundaries, the silence of Khaos. There was only *Rin*.